W9-DCG-661

Mogens

AND OTHER STORIES

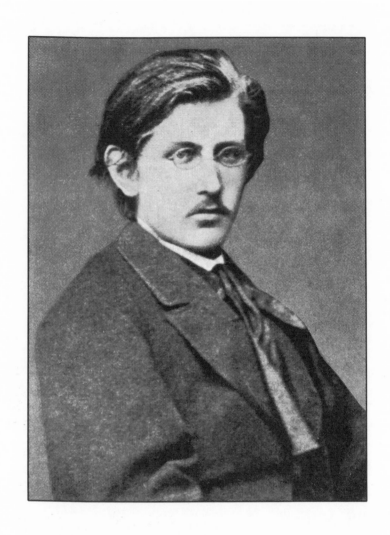

JENS PETER JACOBSEN

Mogens

AND OTHER STORIES

Translated from the Danish
and with an Afterword by
Tiina Nunnally

Fjord Modern Classics No. 5

Fjord Press
Seattle

This translation is dedicated to the memory of
Anna Birthe Rosenberg, née Carsted ◌

Translation copyright © 1994 by Tiina Nunnally
All rights reserved. No part of this book may be reproduced in any form or stored in any information retrieval medium, except for the purposes of a review, without the written permission of the publisher.

Title of Danish edition: *Mogens og andre Noveller.* Originally published in 1882 by Gyldendalske Boghandels Forlag, Copenhagen.

This edition was translated from the definitive edition in the Danish Classics series of the Danish Language and Literature Association, edited by Jørn Erslev Andersen, published by Borgens Forlag, Copenhagen, in 1993.

Grateful acknowledgment is given to the Augustinus Foundation and the Danish Ministry of Cultural Affairs for their support.

Published and distributed by:
Fjord Press, P.O. Box 16349, Seattle, WA 98116
tel (206) 935-7376 / fax (206) 938-1991 / email fjordpress@aol.com

Editor: Steven T. Murray
Cover design: Jane Fleming / Bonnie Smetts
Cover painting of the author by Ernst Josephson, 1879. Reproduced by permission of the Museum of National History at Frederiksborg Castle.
Design & typography: Fjord Press
Printed by McNaughton & Gunn, Saline, MI

Library of Congress Cataloging in Publication Data:

Jacobsen, J. P. (Jens Peter), 1847–1885.
    [Mogens og andre noveller. English]
    Mogens and other stories / Jens Peter Jacobsen ; translated from the Danish and with an afterword by Tiina Nunnally. — 1st ed.
        p.   cm. — (Fjord modern classics ; no. 5)
    Contents: Mogens — A shot in the fog — Two worlds — There should have been roses — The plague in Bergamo — Fru Fønss.
    ISBN 0-940242-58-3 : $24.00. — ISBN 0-940242-57-5 (pbk.) : $12.00
    I. Title.   II. Series.
PT8140.M6E5   1994
839.8'136 — dc20   94-4233
                                                                         CIP

Printed on acid-free paper in the United States of America
First edition

Contents

Mogens

AND OTHER STORIES

Mogens

Summer it was, in the middle of the day, at a corner of the preserve. Opposite stood an old oak tree, and it might well be said that its trunk was writhing in despair at the lack of harmony between its quite new yellow-hued foliage and its gnarled, thick black branches, which more than anything else resembled crudely drawn, ancient Gothic arabesques. Behind the oak there was a luxuriant thicket of hazel shrubs with dark, dull leaves so dense that neither trunks nor branches could be seen. Above the hazel thicket rose two joyous, straight sycamore trees with gaily notched leaves, red stalks, and long baubles of green fruit clusters. Beyond the sycamores the woods began—a green, evenly rounded slope where birds darted in and out like elves from a grassy barrow mound.

All this was visible as you came along the meadow path outside the fence. If you were lying in the shadow of the oak, however, with your back against its trunk and looking the other way—and there was someone doing just that—the first thing you saw would be your own legs, then a little patch of short, thick grass, a large clump of dark nettles, then the hawthorn hedge with the big white convolvulus flowers, the stile, part of the rye field outside, and finally the Councilor's flagpole on the distant hill, and then the sky.

It was oppressively hot, the air shimmered with heat, and it was so quiet. The leaves hung sleeping on the trees; nothing moved except the ladybugs over on the nettles and a few withered leaves that lay on the grass, curling up with abrupt little movements as if they were shrinking beneath the rays of the sun.

And the man under the oak tree; he lay there sighing and gazing mournfully, helplessly up at the sky. He hummed a bit and gave it up, whistled, then gave that up too, turned over, turned over again, and rested his eyes on an old molehill that had been turned a dusty gray by the dry spell. Suddenly a little round dark spot appeared on the light gray soil, then another, a third, fourth, more and still more; the entire mound had turned dark gray. The air was all long dark streaks, the leaves nodded and swayed, and there was a rushing sound that turned to seething; water poured down.

Everything glinted, sparkled, spluttered. Leaves, branches, trunks, everything glistened with wetness; each little drop that fell on the ground, on the grass, on the stile, on anything at all, split and scattered in thousands of tiny beads. Here and there little drops hung on and became larger drops, dripped down, joined with other drops, turned into small streams, vanished into narrow furrows, rushed into big holes and out of small ones, sailed away with dust, with splinters and fragments of leaves, depositing them on land, setting them afloat, spinning them around, and putting them ashore once more. Leaves that had not been together since they were in a bud were reunited by the wetness; moss that had shrunk to nothing in the dry weather swelled up and grew soft, fuzzy, green, and succulent; and gray lichen that had almost turned to snuff unfolded in elaborate lobes, flaring like brocade and with the sheen of silk. The convolvuluses let their white crowns be filled to the brim, they toasted each other and poured the water onto the heads of the nettles. The fat black forest snails blithely squirmed along with a glance of acknowledgment toward the sky. And the man? The man was standing bare-headed in the midst of the downpour, letting the drops run down into his hair and eyebrows, his eyes, nose, and mouth as he snapped his fingers at the rain, occasionally picking up his feet slightly, as if he were about to dance, now and then shaking his head when too much water collected in his hair, and singing at the top of his lungs without realizing what it was he sang, he was so engrossed in the rain:

Had I, oh had I a grandson, oh yes!
And a chest full of many, many coins,
Then I would have a daughter too, oh yes!
And a hearth and home, meadows and fields.

Had I, oh had I a small daughter, oh yes!
And a hearth and home, meadows and fields,
Then I would have a sweetheart too, oh yes!
And chests full of many, many coins.

There he stood, singing, while over among the dark hazel shrubs a girl's head appeared. One long end of her red silk shawl had become tangled in a branch protruding a little farther than the rest, and every now and then a small hand would tug at the end, leading to nothing more than a brief shower from the branch and its neighbors. The rest of the shawl was pulled tight, framing the girl's face; it hid half her forehead and shadowed her eyes, then twisted abruptly and was lost among the leaves, reappearing in a large rosette of folds beneath her chin. The girl's face looked astonished but on the verge of laughter; a smile was already in her eyes. All at once the man who was standing there singing in the rain took a couple of steps to the side, noticed the red silk, the face, the large brown eyes, the tiny, astonished, open mouth; immediately his stance became embarrassed, he looked down at himself in amazement; but at that very moment there was a little shriek, the branch that stuck out swayed violently, the red silk vanished in a flash, the girl's face was gone, and there was a rustling farther and farther inside the hazel shrubs. Then he ran. He did not know why, he did not think at all, the merriment of the rainstorm welled up inside him again, and he ran after the girl's face. It did not occur to him that he was running after a person, it was *merely* a girl's face. He ran, there was a rustle on the right, a rustle on the left, a rustle in front, a rustle in back, he rustled, she rustled, and all that noise and the run itself made him excited, and he called out: "Give a peep, wherever you are!" No one peeped. The sound of his own shouting made him rather uneasy, but still he ran; then one thought arose, but only one, and he muttered as he kept on running: "What will you say to her? What will you say to her?" He headed toward a large bush; *that's* where she was hiding, he could see a scrap of her dress. "What will you say to her? What will you say to her?" he kept mumbling as he ran. He reached the bush, turned sharply, and ran on, muttering the same thing, came out onto a wide path, ran down it a little way, stopped abruptly and burst out laughing; he walked on calmly a bit farther, smiling, and then laughed with all his might, and he continued in this way through the entire preserve.

CR   CR   CR

It was a lovely autumn day, the falling leaves were at
their peak, and the path down to the lake was completely covered with the lemon-yellow leaves of the
elm and the sycamore; here and there were spots of
darker leaves as well. It was pleasant to walk so deco-
rously on this tiger-skin carpet and watch the way the
leaves fell like snow, and the birches looked even more
delicate and lithe with so few leaves on their branches,
and the rowan trees looked so magnificent with their
heavy red clusters of berries. And the sky was so blue,
so blue, and the woods seemed much bigger because
you could see so far into them through the tree trunks.
The fact was that it would all soon be over, the forest,
the meadow, the sky, the fresh air, and everything;
soon it would give way to the time of lamps and car-
pets and potted hyacinths. That's why the Councilor
from "Cape Trafalgar" and his daughter were walking
down toward the lake while the carriage waited for
them at the parish constable's.

The Councilor was a friend of nature. Nature was
utterly unique, nature was one of life's most beautiful
ornaments. The Councilor protected nature, he de-
fended it against the artificial; gardens were nothing
more than corrupted nature, but gardens with style
were nature gone mad. There was no style in nature;
our Lord had assuredly made nature natural, nothing
but natural. Nature was the unrestrained, unspoiled;
but with the Fall, civilization came over human

beings, and now civilization had become a necessity, but it would have been better if it were not; the natural state was something quite different, altogether different. The Councilor would have had nothing against making a living by going around dressed in sheepskins and shooting hare and snipe and plover and grouse and deer and wild boar. No, the natural state was indeed a pearl, a veritable pearl.

The Councilor and his daughter walked down toward the lake. They had been catching glimpses of it through the branches for some time, but now it came into full view as they turned the corner where the big poplar stands. There it was, with large sheets of water clear as a mirror, with serrated tongues of grayish-blue rippling water, with bands that were smooth and bands that were rippled, and the sunlight rested on the smooth areas and flickered on the rippling ones. The water drew their eyes across its surface, led them along its shores by way of softly curving arcs, along abruptly broken lines, swung them around the green promontory, then released their eyes and vanished inside vast bays, while carrying their thoughts with it. Boating! Were there any boats to be hired?

No, there weren't, said a little boy who lived in the white country house and was standing and skipping stones at the shore. Were there no boats at all? Well, yes, there was one; it belonged to the miller, but it was not to be had. The miller wouldn't allow it, the miller's Niels had almost gotten a whipping the last time he lent it out, it was no good even thinking about it. But there was the gentleman who was living at Gamekeeper Nikolai's place, he had an excellent boat, black on top and red on the bottom, and he lent it out to everyone.

The Councilor and his daughter walked up toward Gamekeeper Nikolai's place. Some distance from the house they met a little girl who belonged to Nikolai, and they asked her to run inside to inquire whether they might speak with the gentleman. She ran as if there were trouble, flailing her arms and legs until she reached the door; she put one foot up on the high stoop and fastened her garter, and then she rushed into the house; she reappeared at once with two doors standing open behind her and shouted, before even reaching the stoop again, that the gentleman would come right away. Then she sat down next to the door, leaning against the wall, and peeked up at the strangers from under one arm.

The gentleman appeared; he turned out to be a tall, powerfully built man in his early twenties. The Councilor's daughter was a little shocked when she recognized him as the man who had been singing in the rain. But he looked so pleasant and distracted; it was clear that he had come straight from reading a book, it was evident from the expression in his eyes, from his hair, and from his hands, which had no idea where they were.

The Councilor's daughter curtsied demurely before him, said "Peep," and laughed.

"Peep?" asked the Councilor.

It was that girl's face; the man grew quite red and searched for something to say as the Councilor made an inquiry about the boat. Yes, it was at their disposal. But who would do the rowing? Why, he would, said the young lady, she didn't care what her father said, it didn't matter that it was an inconvenience for the gentleman, for he was not afraid of inconveniencing other people on occasion. Then they walked down to the boat and gave the Councilor an explanation along the way. They were in the boat and a good distance out before the young lady got settled and had time to talk.

"Well," she said, "you were apparently reading something quite learned when I came and peeped you out to sail, weren't you?"

"To row, you mean. Learned! It was the *Story of Knight Peder with the Silver Key and the Beautiful Magelone.*"

"Who is that by?"

"It's not by anyone; that sort of book never is. *Vigoleis and the Golden Wheel* isn't by anyone either, or *Bryde the Archer.*"

"I've never heard those titles before."

"Oh... Would you move over to the other side a little, or the boat won't be level. Well, I'm not surprised; they're not great books, after all, they're the kind you buy at the markets from women hawking stories."

"That's odd; do you always read that sort of book?"

"Always? I don't read many books in general, and I'm actually most fond of the kind that have Indians in them."

"But what about the great works? Oehlen-schläger, Schiller, and the rest?"

"Yes, I know them all right. We had an entire cupboard of them at home, and Frøken Holm—my mother's companion—read aloud from them after lunch and in the evening; but I can't say that I liked them—I don't like verse."

"Don't like verse!... You said 'had'—isn't your mother alive anymore?"

"No, and my father isn't either."

This was said in a rather morose, dismissive tone of voice, and the conversation came to a halt for a while, allowing them to hear clearly the many other sounds produced by the boat's progress through the water.

The young lady broke the silence. "Are you fond of paintings?"

"On altarpieces? Oh, I don't know."

"Yes, or other pictures—landscapes, for instance."

"Do people paint those too? Oh, that's right, of course they do."

"Are you making fun of me?"

"Me? Well, one of us is certainly making fun!"

"But aren't you a student at the university?"

"A student! How could I be a student? No, I'm nothing."

"But you must be something. You must do *something.*"

"Why is that?"

"Because… because everybody does."

"Do you do something?"

"Well, no! But you're no lady."

"No, thank God."

"Thank you very much."

He stopped rowing, raised the oars slightly, looked her in the eye, and said, "What do you mean by that? No, you mustn't be angry with me; I have to tell you that I'm such an odd person. You can't even imagine. You think that because I look like a fine gentleman in these clothes that I must be a fine man. My father was a fine man, and people have told me that he knew such an enormous amount, and he probably did too since he was a high official. I don't know anything, because Mother and I indulged each other in every way, and I never felt like learning what you learn in school, and I still don't. Oh, you should have seen my mother. She was such a tiny, tiny lady; even as a thirteen-year-old I could carry her down to the garden. She weighed so little; during her last years I would often carry her in my arms all around the park and garden. I can see her with her black dresses trimmed with all those pieces of wide lace..."

He grabbed the oars and began rowing vigorously. The Councilor grew rather uneasy when he saw the water rise up so steeply at the stern, and he thought that they ought to see about returning to shore. They turned back.

"Tell me," said the young lady, when the strenuous rowing had slackened a bit, "do you often go into town?"

"I've never been there."

"Never been there! But you live only fifteen miles away."

"I don't live here all the time. I've lived all sorts of places since Mother died, but this winter I'll be going to town to learn to calculate."

"Mathematics?"

"No, lumber," he said, laughing. "You probably don't understand. Well, let me tell you: When I'm twenty-five and come of age, I'm going to buy a sloop and sail to Norway, and I'll need to be able to do accounts for customs clearance."

"Is that what you really want to do?"

"Oh, being at sea is splendid, sailing is so full of life—well, here's the pier."

He docked the boat; the Councilor and his daughter stepped ashore after procuring his promise to stop by and visit them at "Cape Trafalgar." Then they walked up to the parish constable's house, while he rowed out across the lake. Up by the poplar tree they could still hear the strokes of the oars.

CR   CR   CR

"Kamilla," said the Councilor, who had been out to lock the front door. "Tell me," he said as he put out his candlestick with the bit of his key, "was that rose they had at Karlsen's called a Pompadour or a Maintenon?"

"A Cendrillon," replied his daughter.

"That's right, that's what it was... Well—I suppose we'd better see about going to bed. Goodnight, my dear. Goodnight and sleep well."

When Kamilla reached her room she rolled up the shade, leaned her forehead against the cold window-pane, and hummed "Elisabeth's Song" from *Elverhøj*. At sunset a light breeze had come up and, illuminated by the moon, a few small white clouds hastened toward Kamilla. She stood watching them for a long time, following them from a great distance and humming louder and louder the closer they came, falling silent for a few seconds as they vanished overhead, then seeking out new ones and following them. With a little sigh she rolled down the shade once again. She went over to the dressing table and rested her elbows on it, leaned her head on her folded hands, and looked in the mirror at her image without actually seeing it.

She was thinking about a tall young man walking around with a little invalid woman dressed in black in his arms; she was thinking about a tall young man steering a small vessel through the rocks and skerries in a raging storm. She heard the entire conversation over again. She blushed: Eugen Karlsen would have thought you were flirting with him. With a little jealous association of ideas she continued: Klara would never have let someone run after her in the rain out in the woods; and on top of that she would never have summoned a stranger—outright *summoned* him—to go boating with her. "A lady to the tips of her fingers," Karlsen had said about Klara, that was a reprimand to you, my little peasant girl Kamilla. Then she undressed with affected slowness, got into bed, took a small, elegant book from the *étagère* next to the bed, opened it to the first page and read a little handwritten poem with a tired, bitter expression, let the book fall to the floor, and burst into tears. Then she gently picked up the book, put it back in its place, and put out the light; she lay there for a while, staring inconsolably at the moonlit windowshade, and finally fell asleep.

Only a few days later the "man in the rain" set off for "Cape Trafalgar." He met a farmer driving a cart of rye straw and was allowed to ride along. He lay on his back in the straw and looked up at the cloudless sky.

For the first two miles he lay there letting his thoughts
come and go as they pleased; they were not particu-
larly varied, however. Most of them wondered how a
person could be so unbelievably beautiful, astounded
that he could amuse himself for several days simply by
recalling the features of a face, its expressions and
changes in hue, the small movements of a head and a
pair of hands, and the shifting tone of a voice. But then
the farmer pointed his whip at a slate roof a mile off
and told him it was the Councilor's, and the good
Mogens sat up in the straw and stared uneasily at the
rooftop; he had a strange feeling of anxiety, and he
tried to imagine that no one was home, but he was
stubbornly drawn to the notion that they had many
visitors today, and he could not get rid of this idea no
matter how many cows he counted that "Landlyst"
had put out to graze, or how many piles of gravel he
could see along the road. After a while the farmer
stopped where a narrow lane led out to the country
house, and Mogens slid down from the cart and set
about brushing off the pieces of straw as the cart
slowly crunched off down the gravel road. Mogens
approached the garden gate tentatively and noticed a
red shawl vanish behind the balcony windows, a small
white sewing basket abandoned on the balcony railing, and the swaying back of an empty rocking chair.
He stepped into the garden with his gaze still fixed on
the balcony, heard the Councilor say "Good day,"

turned his head toward the sound, and saw him standing there, nodding, with his arms full of empty flowerpots. They chatted for a while, and then the Councilor
started to expound on the fact that in some ways one
might say that the old classification differences for the
various species of trees had been eliminated by graft-
ing, something to which he was strictly opposed, by
the way. Then Kamilla came slowly toward them,
wearing a brilliant blue shawl. She had her arms
wrapped in the shawl and greeted him with a slight
nod of her head and a muted "Welcome." The Councilor left with his flowerpots; Kamilla stood looking
over her shoulder at the balcony; Mogens looked at
her. How had he been since the other day? Yes, well,
he had been fine, he supposed. Had he been out rowing much? Oh, about the same as usual, maybe not
quite as much. She turned her face toward him, looked
at him coldly, tilted her head a little to one side, and
asked him with half-closed eyes and a feeble smile
whether it was the beautiful Magelone who had been
monopolizing him. He didn't know what she meant,
but he supposed she might be right. Then they stood
there for a while without saying a word. Kamilla took
a few steps toward a corner with a bench and a garden
chair. She sat down on the bench and, after she was
seated, looked at the chair and suggested that he sit
down; he must be tired after the long, long walk. He
sat down on the chair.

Did he think anything would come of the intended betrothal? Perhaps it didn't interest him? Of course he didn't care about the royal family, did he? He hated the aristocracy, of course. There were very few young gentlemen who didn't think that democracy was God only knows what. He was no doubt one of those who placed no political importance on the family relationships of the royal house. But he could very well be mistaken. Of course, there was the fact that.... She stopped abruptly, surprised that Mogens— who at first had seemed rather taken aback by all this —now looked thoroughly amused. He wasn't going to sit there laughing at her, was he? She turned quite red.

"Are you very interested in politics?" she asked anxiously.

"Not in the least."

"Then why are you letting me sit here and go on and on about politics?"

"Oh, you say everything so beautifully that it doesn't matter what you talk about."

"That's not much of a compliment."

"Oh, but it *is*," he assured her earnestly, since he thought she looked so offended.

Kamilla burst out laughing, jumped up, and ran to meet her father, taking his arm and escorting him over to the astonished Mogens.

After dinner was over and they had had coffee up on the balcony, the Councilor suggested a walk. All three of them strolled down the little lane, across the main highway, and along a narrow path where there was rye stubble on either side, over the stile, and into the preserve. There stood the oak and everything else; there were even convolvuluses still in the hawthorn thicket. Kamilla asked Mogens to pick some of them for her. He tore off all of them and came back with a whole handful.

"Thank you, but I don't need so many," she said, taking a few of them and letting the rest fall to the ground.

"Then I wish I had let them be," said Mogens gravely.

Kamilla bent down and started gathering them up. She expected him to help her and looked up at him in surprise, but he stood there quite calmly gazing down at her. Well, since she had started this she might as well finish, and she picked up all of them; but then she certainly did not speak to Mogens for a long, long time; she did not even look in his direction. But they must have been reconciled, for when they once again reached the oak on their way home, Kamilla went over to it and looked up into its crown, prancing from side to side and throwing out her hands and singing, and Mogens had to go over to the hazel shrubs to see what he had looked like. Suddenly Kamilla ran toward him, but Mogens stepped out of his role and forgot to scream and run, and then Kamilla declared with a laugh that she was very disappointed with herself and that she had not thought she would be bold enough to stay put when such a terrible person—and here she pointed at herself—came rushing toward her. But Mogens declared that he was quite satisfied with himself.

Toward sunset, when it was time to go home, the Councilor and Kamilla accompanied him part of the way. And as they walked homeward, she said to her father that they probably ought to invite that lonely man over more often during the month they still contemplated staying in the country, for he knew no one at all out here, and the Councilor said yes, and smiled at being taken for so ingenuous, but Kamilla walked on, looking gently somber so there could be no doubt that she was empathy personified.

The autumn weather was so mild now that the Councilor and his daughter stayed at "Cape Trafalgar" an entire month, and Kamilla's sympathy led to Mogens coming to visit twice in the first week and almost every day by the third.

It was one of the last days of good weather; it had rained early in the morning and had been overcast until almost noon, but now the sun had come out, shining so strong and hot that the wet garden paths, the lawns, and the branches of the trees were swathed in a fine, light mist. The Councilor was cutting asters; Mogens and Kamilla were over in a corner of the

garden picking some late fall apples. He was standing
on top of a table with a basket over his arm, she was
standing on a chair holding the corners of a big white
apron.

"So what happened then?" she shouted impatiently at Mogens, who had broken off the fairy tale he
was telling her so he could reach an apple hanging up
high.

"Well," he went on, "then the farmer began to
spin around three times and sing: 'To Babylon! To
Babylon! With an iron ring through my skull.' And
then he and his heifer and his great-grandmother and
his black rooster started flying; they flew over seas as
wide as Arup Marsh, over mountains as high as Jan-
nerup Church, over Himmerland, and all the way
south through Holstein to the ends of the earth. There
sat the troll eating breakfast; he had just finished when
they arrived.

" 'You should be a little more God-fearing, old
man,' said the farmer, 'or you might walk right past
Heaven.'

"Yes, he would like to be God-fearing.

" 'Then you must say the benediction,' said the
farmer... Oh, I don't feel like telling any more," said
Mogens impatiently.

"All right, don't," said Kamilla, looking at him in
surprise.

"I might as well say it right now," Mogens continued. "I want to ask you something, but you mustn't laugh at me."

Kamilla jumped down from the chair.

"Tell me... No, I want to tell *you* something," said Mogens. "Here's the table and there's the fence. If you don't want to be my sweetheart, then I'll take off with the basket over that fence and be gone. One."

Kamilla peeked up at him and saw the smile disappear from his face.

"Two."

He was quite pale with emotion.

"Yes," she whispered, letting go of the corners of her apron so the apples tumbled in all directions, and then she ran.

But she did not run away from Mogens.

"Three," she said, when he reached her, but he kissed her all the same.

The Councilor was disturbed among his asters, but the official's son was a much too exemplary combination of nature and civilization for the Councilor to think of raising any objections.

   ᬯ ᬯ ᬯ

It was near the end of winter; the heavy, thick layer of snow, the result of a full week of continual drifting, was rapidly melting away. The air was full of sunshine and reflections from the white snow, which dripped past the windows in big glittering drops. Inside the parlor all manner of colors had been awakened, all contours and silhouettes seemed alive: flat surfaces spread out, curved ones curled up, diagonals slipped, and jagged ones disintegrated. Every green nuance swirled together on the table with the flowers, from the softest dark green to the sharpest yellow-green. Brownish-red hues flowed in flames over the surface of the mahogany table, and gold glittered and sparkled from knick-knacks and frames and moldings, but on the carpet all the colors broke into a festive, shining tumult.

Kamilla was sitting at the window, sewing, and she and the Graces on the console table were completely enveloped in a reddish glow from the red drapes, and Mogens, who was slowly pacing the floor, kept passing in and out of slanting bands of light with faintly rainbow-hued dust.

He was in a talkative mood.

"That's certainly an odd group of people, the ones you associate with," he said. "There's not a thing between heaven and earth that they can't finish off with a wave of the hand: this is base and that is noble; this is the stupidest thing since the creation of the world, and that is the cleverest; one thing is so ugly, so very ugly, while the other is so inexpressibly lovely; and they all agree on everything, as though they had a specific chart or something they used to figure it out, because they all come up with the same result, no matter what it is. How alike they are, those people! They all know the same things and talk the same way, they all have the same words and the same opinions."

"You don't really think that Karlsen and Rønholt share the same opinions, do you?" objected Kamilla.

"Oh, they're the loveliest of the lot. They belong to different parties. Their basic views are as different as night and day! No, they're not, they're so similar that it's a joy when there happens to be some little detail they can actually disagree about. It might be only a misunderstanding, but God help me if it isn't sheer comedy to listen to them. They seem to have agreed to do everything possible to disagree; they start by shouting out loud, then they talk themselves into a tizzy, then in a fit of temper one of them says something he doesn't mean, then the other one says the exact opposite, which he doesn't mean either, and then the first one attacks what the second doesn't mean and the second one attacks what the first doesn't mean, and then the game is on."

"But what have they ever done to you?"

"They annoy me, those fellows. When you look them in the eye, it seems you're almost guaranteed that from now on nothing extraordinary will ever happen in the world."

Kamilla put down her sewing, went over and took hold of the corners of his lapels, and looked up at him with an archly inquisitive glance.

"I can't stand that Karlsen," he grumbled, tossing his head.

"I see. And?..."

"And you are so sweet, so very sweet," he murmured, comically affectionate.

"And?"

"And," he bristled, "he looks at you and listens to you and talks to you in a way that I don't like; he has to stop it, he must, because you are *mine* and not *his*. Isn't that true? You *aren't* his, not at all. You are *mine*, you have pledged yourself to *me*, like Doctor Faust did to the Devil, you are mine in body and soul, every inch of you, totally and for all eternity."

She nodded to him rather anxiously, looked up at him devotedly; her eyes filled with tears and she hid herself against him, and he threw his arms around her, bent down to her, and kissed her on the forehead.

In the evening of that same day, Mogens accompanied the Councilor to the post chaise; unexpected orders had arrived for the Councilor informing him of an official journey he had to make. The next morning Kamilla was to go out to her aunt's house and stay there until he returned.

After Mogens had bid his future father-in-law farewell, he walked home, thinking about the fact that he would not see Kamilla for several days. He turned down the street where she lived. It was long and narrow with very little traffic. A carriage rumbled away at the far end of the street; down there he could also hear the sound of retreating footsteps. Now he heard only the barking of a dog inside the building behind him. He looked up at the house where Kamilla lived: it was dark on the ground floor, as usual, and the whitewashed windowpanes were only slightly enlivened by the flickering glow of the lamp on the building next door. On the third floor the windows stood open, and in one of them a full dozen boards stuck out over the windowsill. Kamilla's room was dark, the floor above was dark, only in a single attic window was there a whitish-gold glow from the moon. Above the house the clouds were in wild flight. In the buildings on either side the windows were illuminated.

The dark house made Mogens melancholy, it stood there so abandoned and disconsolate; the hooks of the open windows rattled, the water ran down the rainspout, drumming monotonously; every now and then a little water would fall somewhere he couldn't see with a hollow, soft sound, and the wind rushed heavily through the street. That dark, dark house! Mogens' eyes filled with tears, his chest felt tight, and a strange, gloomy feeling came over him that he was

somehow at fault for something concerning Kamilla.
Then he happened to think of his mother and felt a
longing to put his head in her lap and sob his heart out.

He stood like that for a long time, his hand
pressed to his breast, until a carriage came driving at a
brisk trot down the street; then he turned in the same
direction and walked home. He had to tug at the door
for a long time before it opened; then he ran, humming, up the stairs, and when he was inside, he threw
himself onto the sofa with one of Smollett's novels in
his hand and read and laughed until past midnight.

Finally it grew too cold in the room; he jumped
up and stomped back and forth to chase the cold away.
He stopped at the window: one side of the sky was so
bright that the snow-covered rooftops melted into it;
in the other direction several long clouds were sailing
by, and beneath them the air had an oddly reddish
tinge, an unsteady rippling glow, a smoldering red
haze; he flung open the window, there was a fire over
near the Councilor's house. Down the stairs, along the
street as fast as he could; down a cross street, through
a side street, and then straight ahead; he could see
nothing yet, but when he turned the corner he saw the
fiery red glow. A couple of dozen people were pounding along the street. As they ran past each other they
asked where the fire was. The reply was: the refinery.
Mogens kept running as fast as ever, but his heart was
greatly relieved. Several more streets; more and more

people appeared, and they were talking about the soap
factory. It lay right across the street from the
Councilor's house. Mogens ran like a madman. There
was only one diagonal cross street left, it was completely filled with people: calm, well-dressed gentlemen; old women in rags who stood there talking in a
drawling, whimpering tone of voice; shouting appren-
tices; girls all decked out, whispering to each other;
bounders who stood around telling jokes; befuddled
drunkards and drunkards arguing; helpless police
officers; and carriages that could move neither back
nor forward. Mogens squeezed through the crowd.
Now he had reached the corner; sparks were drifting
slowly down on him. Up the street; sparks flew, windowpanes glowed on both sides, the factory was on
fire, the Councilor's house was on fire, and the building next door was on fire too. It was all smoke, fire,
and confusion, shouts, curses, roof tiles clattering
down, axes chopping, wood splintering, windows
shattering, streams of water whistling, sputtering, and
splashing, and in the midst of it all the rhythmic,
muffled sobbing of the pump. Furniture, bedclothes,
black helmets, ladders, shiny buttons, faces lit up,
wheels, ropes, sailcloth, strange-looking equipment;
Mogens plunged through, over, and under it all, on-
ward to the house.

The façade was brightly lit by flames from the
burning factory, smoke trickled out between the roof

tiles and poured out of the open windows on the second floor; inside, the fire crackled and roared; there
was a slow crashing sound that turned into rumbling
and creaking and ended with a hollow roar; smoke,
sparks, and flames were forced violently out of all the
openings in the building, and then the flames began to
flicker and crack with twice the strength and twice the
brightness. It was the center section of the second-
floor ceiling that had fallen in. With both hands
Mogens grabbed a tall fire ladder that was leaning up
against the part of the factory not yet in flames. For a
moment it stood vertical, but then it fell away from
him against the Councilor's house, bashing in a window frame up on the third floor. Mogens raced up the
ladder and in through the opening. At first he had to
close his eyes to the piercing wood smoke; and the
heavy, suffocating fumes rising up from the charred
timbers, which the streams of water had managed to
reach, robbed him of breath. He was in the dining
room. The wall next to the parlor had virtually collapsed. The parlor was a great, smoldering abyss, every
now and then the flames from down in the depths of
the house would reach almost to the ceiling; and the
few slats that were left hanging when the floor collapsed were burning with clear whitish-yellow flames;
shadows and the glare of the fire rippled across the
walls; here and there the wallpaper curled up, ignited,
and fell in fiery scraps down into the depths; and

nimble yellow flames licked up along loose moldings
and picture frames. Mogens crawled over rubble and
debris from the collapsed wall to the edge of the pit;
from down below, currents of air shifting from cold to
hot billowed up toward his face; over on the other side,
so much of the wall had caved in that he could look
right into Kamilla's room, while the section hiding the
Councilor's office was still standing. It grew hotter
and hotter. The skin on his face tightened, and he
could feel his hair starting to curl. Something heavy
brushed past his shoulder and came to rest on his back,
forcing him to the floor; it was the trimming joist
which had slowly slipped down from its place. He
could not move, his breathing grew more and more
strained, and his temples were pounding violently; to
his left a stream of water was splashing against the
outer wall of the dining room, and he became obsessed
with the desire for those cold, cold drops spreading in
every direction to spatter over onto him. Then he
heard a groan from the other side of the pit, and he saw
something white moving on the floor of Kamilla's
room. It was her. She was on her knees, holding one
hand to either side of her head as she swayed back and
forth at the hips. She stood up slowly and approached
the edge of the abyss. She stood rigidly erect, her arms
hanging limply at her sides, her head seemed to
wobble on her neck; slowly, very slowly, she bent forward at the waist; her lovely long hair swept the

floor—a sudden, brilliant flash, and it was gone; in the next instant she pitched headlong into the flames.

Mogens let out a wailing sound, abrupt, deep, and wrenching, like the roar of a wild beast, and at the same moment he made a violent effort to move away from the chasm, but he could not because of the joist; his hands fumbled over the fragments of brick, then seemed to freeze in a fierce grip around them, and then he began to bang his forehead rhythmically against the rubble, moaning: Dear *God*, dear *God*, dear *God*!

He lay that way for some time until he noticed that something was grabbing him; it was a fireman, who had thrown the joist aside and was now attempting to carry him out of the building; with a strong feeling of foreboding Mogens felt himself lifted up and carried away. The fireman took him over to the opening; it was then that Mogens had a clear sense that harm had been done him, and that the fireman carrying him wanted to kill him; he tore himself out of his arms, seized hold of a lath lying on the floor, struck the fireman on the head with it so he toppled backwards, went out the opening and ran upright down the ladder, holding the lath over his head. Through the tumult, the smoke, the crowd of people, down empty streets, across deserted squares, out into a field. Deep snow everywhere, a short distance away a black patch, it was a gravel heap sticking up above the layer of snow, he struck it with the lath, hit it again and again,

kept on hitting it, he wanted to club it to death, so that
it disappeared altogether, he wanted to run far away,
so he ran around it, swinging at it like a madman, but
it would not disappear, it refused to disappear, he
flung the lath far away and threw himself on top of the
black heap to obliterate it, his hands were full of small
stones, it was gravel, it was a black heap of gravel; why
was he lying out here in the field tearing at a heap of
black gravel? He smelled the smoke, the flames flickered around him, he saw Kamilla plunge into them, he
screamed and raced across the field. He could not get
rid of the sight of those flames, he covered his eyes
with his hands: flames, flames! threw himself to the
ground and pressed his face into the snow: flames!
leapt up, ran back, ran forward, turned around: flames
everywhere; took off across the snow past the buildings, past trees, past a terrified face staring out a window, around haystacks and through barnyards where
dogs howled and tore at their chains. He ran around
the wing of a farmhouse and suddenly stood before a
window brightly and erratically lit, the light did him
good, the flames receded; he went over to the window
and looked inside, it was a scullery, a girl was standing
by the hearth stirring a kettle; the light she held in her
hand shone dimly red in the thick haze, another girl
was sitting there plucking poultry, and a third was
singeing them over the big flames of a fire made with
long thatching; the flames died down, then new straw

was added, and they flared up again, then they grew smaller, still smaller, and died out. Mogens angrily shattered a windowpane with his elbow and slowly drifted away, the girls inside screamed. Then he started running again, ran for a long time, quietly whimpering. Scattered glimpses of memories from the good times came to him, and it all seemed doubly dark when they vanished, he couldn't stand thinking about what had happened, it could not have happened, he threw himself to his knees and wrung his hands at the heavens as he pleaded for what had happened to be undone. For a long time he dragged himself along on his knees, keeping his eyes fixed on the sky, as if he feared that it might slip away and avoid his prayers if he did not keep looking at it. Then images from the good times appeared, floating, more and more of them, in dim rows in the fog; there were other images that shot up around him with sudden radiance, and others swung past so blurred, so distant, that they were gone before he even recognized what they were. He sat quietly in the snow, mesmerized by light and color, by life and happiness; and the vague fear he had had in the beginning, that something might come and extinguish it all, was gone. It was so quiet around him, so calm inside him, the images had vanished, but the joy remained. So quiet! There was not a sound; but sounds can haunt. And laughter and songs came, and

lighthearted words came, and light footsteps and the
hollow sobbing of the pump throbs. Whimpering, he
ran off, ran on and on, reached the lake and followed
its banks until the root of a tree brought him down,
and since he was so weary, he stayed there on the
ground.

With a gentle gurgling sound the water splashed
over the gravel, sporadically the wind sighed lightly in
the naked branches, a few crows shrieked from across
the lake, and the morning cast its harsh blue light over
the woods and the lake, over the snow and over the
pale face.

At dawn he was found by the forest warden from
the neighboring woods and was carried up to Gamekeeper Nikolai's, and there he lay for days and weeks,
hovering between life and death.

At about the time that Mogens was being taken up to
Nikolai's, there was a commotion around a carriage at
the end of the street where the Councilor lived. The
driver could not understand why the police officer was
preventing him from going about his lawful business,
and that is what they were fighting about. It was the
carriage that was to have taken Kamilla to her aunt's.

ʒ   ʒ   ʒ

"No! Ever since poor Kamilla came to such a sad end, we haven't seen a trace of him."

"Yes, it's strange what can be concealed inside a man. No one suspected a thing. So proper and reserved, almost awkward. Isn't that so, madam, you didn't suspect a thing, did you?"

"About the sickness? Dear God, how can you ask such a thing! Oh, you mean... I didn't understand your question... that there was supposedly something in his blood, something inherited? Yes, I remember there was something about his father being taken off to Aarhus. Isn't that true, Herr Karlsen?"

"No! Well, yes, but that was to the cemetery, that's where his first wife is buried. No, I was thinking about, you know, the terrible... well, the terrible life he has led for the past two or two and a half years."

"Oh, I see, no... no... No! I don't know anything about that."

"Yes... well... it's not the kind of thing one likes to talk about, one doesn't like to... well! You understand; out of respect for the relatives. The Councilor's family...."

"What you say *does* have some justification, of course—but, on the other hand—tell me quite honestly, don't you think that nowadays there's a false, a... pietistic striving to veil, to disguise the weaknesses of our fellow human beings? And—of course, I don't have much understanding of such things—but don't

you think that the truth or the public morals, and I
don't mean morality but morals, or the human condition, or what have you, suffer from this?"

"Quite right! And I am most eminently pleased to
agree with you, and in this instance... The fact is that
he has given himself over to excesses of every possible
kind, he has lived in the most spineless manner with
the basest rabble, people without honor, without con-
science, without position, religion or anything else,
drifters, carnival performers, carousers, and... and, if
the truth be told: loose women."

"And after being engaged to Kamilla; God in
Heaven. And after having suffered from brain fever
for three months!"

"Yes... and what might that imply about certain
tendencies, and I wonder what his past was like, what
do you think?"

"And God only knows how things really stood
during their betrothal. He *was* rather secretive. At
least that's *my* opinion."

"Pardon me, madam, and pardon me as well, Herr
Karlsen. You're discussing the whole thing rather abstractly, quite abstractly. I happen to have concrete
reports from a friend over in Jutland and can present
all the details of this matter."

"Herr Rønholt! You wouldn't...."

"Reveal the details? Yes, of course I would, Herr
Karlsen, with the lady's permission. Thank you. It's

true he has not lived in the manner one ought to after
a brain fever. He's been roaming through the markets
with a couple of drinking companions, and he hasn't
refrained from contact with riffraff and peddlers,
and—as we feared and now know—with troupes of
artistes, and their female members in particular. Perhaps it would make more sense if I ran upstairs and got
my friend's letter. If you will permit me? It won't take
a moment."

"Don't you think that Rønholt is especially ami-
able today, Herr Karlsen?"

"Yes! Indubitably, but madam must also keep in
mind that he released all his venom in an article in this
morning's paper. Imagine daring to propose... It's
outright insurrection, contempt for the law, for...
hmm...."

"Did you find the letter?"

"Yes, I did. May I begin? Now let me see—oh yes:
'Our mutual friend, whom we met last year in Møn-
sted, and whom you said you knew from Copenhagen, has been residing here in the area for the past few
months. He looks just the same as he did then, he's the
same pale, sad knight of the sorrowful countenance.
He's the most peculiar mixture of forced liveliness and
quiet despair; he's deliberately inconsiderate and bru-
tal toward himself and others, he's silent and taciturn,
and he doesn't seem to enjoy himself although he does
nothing but carouse; it's the same as I said then, he's

obsessed with the idea that he has been personally in-
sulted by life. His companions here have been a horse
dealer known as the Pub Deacon because he's always
singing and always on a binge; and a raffish, gawky
cross between a sailor and a peddler, known and feared
under the name of Per Out-of-Control; as well as
Pretty Abelone, although lately she has had to yield
her position to a dark female belonging to a group of
acrobats who have entertained us for some time now
with feats of strength and tightrope walking. You've
seen those kinds of women, with pinched, jaundiced
faces prematurely aged; women destroyed by brutal-
ity, poverty, and wretched vices and who always wear
excessive amounts of moth-eaten velvet and smudged
rouge. So that's his group of companions. I can't understand our friend's passion; certainly it's true that
his sweetheart came to a sorrowful end, but that
doesn't explain matters. And I have to tell you how he
left us. We were at a market several miles from here;
he was sitting with Out-of-Control, the horse dealer,
and that female in a tent serving as a pub, and they
caroused late into the night. At three in the morning
or so they were finally ready to leave. They went out
to the wagon, and things were going fine, but then our
mutual friend turns off the highway and takes off with
them across the fields and heath, as fast as the horses
can run, the wagon lunging from one side to the other.
Finally it's too much for the horse dealer, and he

shouts that he wants to get out. After he gets down,
our mutual friend whips up the horses again and heads
straight for a big heath-covered hill; then the woman
gets scared and climbs down; now they start up the hill
and down the other side in such a wild rush that it's a
miracle the wagon doesn't reach the bottom ahead of
the horses. In the meantime, on the way up, Per had
sneaked out of the wagon, and as thanks for the ride he
threw his big jackknife at the driver's head.' "

"That poor man! But it *is* awful about that
woman."

"Despicable, madam, thoroughly despicable. Do
you really think that this report is supposed to show
this man in a better light, Herr Rønholt?"

"No, but in a more precise one; you know how
easy it is in the dark to assume things are larger than
they are."

"Can anything worse be imagined?"

"If not, then this is the worst; but you know, you
never ought to think the worst of anyone."

"So you think the whole thing is actually not so
terrible, that there's something invigorating about it
all, something plebeian in the highest sense of the
word, which appeals to your penchant for things
democratic?"

"Don't you see that he's behaving quite aristocratically toward the people around him?"

"Aristocratically! Well, this certainly is a paradox. If he's not democratic, then I don't know what he is."

"Well, other matters do come into play here."

White bird-cherries, bluish lilacs, red hawthorn, and brilliant laburnum were fragrantly blooming outside the house. The windows stood open, with the blinds rolled down. Mogens was leaning in over the window-sill, with the blind resting on his back. It was soothing to the eye to be looking into the parlor's dim, soft, calm light after all that summer sunshine on the woods and the water and in the air. A tall, voluptuous woman was standing inside with her back to the window, putting flowers in a large vase. The bodice of her rose-colored morning dress was gathered high up under her breasts with a shiny black leather belt; on the floor behind her lay a snow-white dressing gown; her thick, very blonde hair was caught up in a bright red hairnet.

"You're quite pale after the carousing yesterday," was the first thing Mogens said.

"Good morning," she replied, and without turning around she held out her hand toward him with the flowers she was holding. Mogens took one of the flowers. Laura turned her head halfway around, opened her hand slightly, and let the flowers fall in little bunches to the floor. Then she returned to her fussing with the vase.

"Feeling ill?" asked Mogens.

"Tired."

"I won't be eating lunch with you today."

"You won't!"

"We can't eat dinner together either."

"Are you going fishing?"

"No! Goodbye!"

"When will you be back?"

"I'm not coming back."

"What do you mean by that?" she asked, as she straightened her dress, came over to the window, and sat down on a chair.

"I'm tired of you. That's all."

"Now you're being mean. What's wrong? What have I done?"

"Nothing, but since we're neither married nor madly in love with each other, I can't see anything strange about leaving."

"Are you jealous?" she asked quite softly.

"Over someone like you? Lord preserve my sanity!"

"What's the meaning of all this?"

"It means that I'm tired of your beauty, that I know your voice and your gestures by heart, and that your moods, your stupidity, and your deceit no longer amuse me. So can you give me any reason why I should stay?"

Laura wept. "Mogens, Mogens, how can you do this? Oh, what am I going to do, what am I going to do, what am I going to do? Just stay today, Mogens, just today. You *can't* leave me."

"That's a lie, Laura, you don't even believe it yourself; it's not because you're so terribly fond of me that you're sad; you're just a little disconcerted by a change, you're afraid of a slight disturbance in your daily routine. I know it all so well, you're not the first one I've grown tired of."

"Oh, just stay with me today and I won't beg you to stay even an hour longer."

"You're like dogs, you women! You don't have a scrap of honor in your life; if you're kicked aside, you come crawling back."

"Yes, we do, but just stay today—won't you?—stay!"

"Stay, stay! No!"

"Oh, you've never loved me, Mogens."

"No, I haven't."

"Yes, you have, you loved me that day when the wind was blowing so hard, oh, that exquisite day down by the shore, when we sat in the shelter of the boat."

"Silly girl."

"If only I were a proper girl with rich parents and not who I am, then you'd stay with me, then you wouldn't be so cruel—to me, who loves you so much!"

"You mustn't do that."

"No, I'm like the dust you walk on; that's how

much you care for me. Not one kind word, only harsh ones; contempt is good enough for me."

"The others are no better or worse than you. Goodbye, Laura."

He stretched out his hand to her, but she put her hands behind her back and whimpered: "No, no, not goodbye! Not goodbye!"

Mogens lifted the shade, took a few steps back, and let it drop below the window. Laura quickly ducked under the blind and leaned out the windowsill, pleading: "Come here! Come here and give me your hand."

"No."

When he had gone some distance away, she shouted plaintively, "Goodbye, Mogens."

He turned toward the house with a brief wave. Then he continued on. "And a girl like that still believes in love! No, she *couldn't*."

༄   ༄   ༄

The evening wind blew in from the sea across the countryside, and the lyme grass swung its pale spikes and lifted its pointed leaves slightly, the rushes swayed, the lake in the dunes grew dark with thousands of fine ripples, and the lily pads tugged uneasily on their stalks. Then the heather began waving its dusky tops, and in the sandy fields the sheep sorrel reeled aimlessly. In over the mainland! The sheaves of

oats bowed, the young clover trembled on the stub-
bled field, and the wheat bent from high to low in great
waves, the rooftops yielded, the mill creaked, the
weathervanes spun around, the smoke whirled down
into the chimneys, and dew covered the windowpanes.

There was a rushing in the belfries, in the poplars
by the manor house, and a whistling in the windblown
thicket on Bredbjerg Grønhøj. Mogens was lying up
there and looking out across the dark earth. The moon
was beginning to shine, the mists were drifting past in
the meadow below. All of life was so sad: empty behind, dark up ahead. But that's the way life *was*. Those
who went around happy were also blind. Despair had
taught him to see, everything was unjust and deceitful,
the whole world was one great tumbling lie; loyalty,
friendship, mercy—all lies, every bit a lie; but what
was called love was the hollowest of the hollow, desire
is what it was, burning desire, smoldering desire,
steaming desire, but *desire* and nothing more. Why did
he have to know about this? Why hadn't he been
allowed to keep his faith in all those flame-gilded lies?
Why did he have to see while the others were blind?
He had a right to blindness, he had believed in everything it was possible to believe in.

The lamps were lighted in the town below.

Home upon home was down there. My home!
My home! And my child's faith in all that is wonderful
in the world! And what if they were right, those other
people? What if the world were full of beating hearts,

and the heavens full of a loving God? But why don't I *know* that? Why do I know something different? And I do know something different, so scathing, bitter, and true....

He stood up, both field and meadow lay in full moonlight before him. He walked down toward the town, taking the path along the manor house garden; as he walked he looked in over the stone wall. On a lawn in the garden stood a silver poplar, the moonlight falling brightly on its quaking leaves, which turned first the dark side up and then the light. He propped his elbows on the wall and stared at the tree; it looked as if the leaves were trickling down over the branches. He thought he could hear the sound produced by the foliage. Suddenly a lovely woman's voice sounded nearby:

> *You blossom in the dew!*
> *You blossom in the dew!*
> *Whisper to me the dreams that are thine.*
> *Do they possess that same air,*
> *That very same fairyland air,*
> *As in mine?*
> *And does it whisper, sigh, and lament*
> *Through the dying scent and slumbering glow,*
> *Through awakening clamor, through budding song:*
> *With longing,*
> *With longing I live!*

Then silence returned. Mogens took a deep breath and
listened intently: no song. Up by the estate, he heard a
door close. Now he could clearly hear the sound of the
silver poplar's leaves. He put his head down on his
arms and wept.

The next day was one of those days with which
late summer is so richly endowed. A day with a brisk,
cool breeze, with many large, rapidly passing clouds
and a constant interplay of dark and light as the clouds
skimmed past the sun. Mogens had gone up to the
cemetery; the garden of the manor house was right
next to it. It looked quite bare up there, the grass had
been recently cut; behind an old, rectangular iron
grille stood a wide, low elder shrub fluttering its
leaves. A few of the graves were enclosed with wooden
frames, but most of them were merely low rectangular
mounds; some had tin displays with inscriptions, others had wooden crosses with the paint peeling off, still
others had wax wreaths, most of them had nothing at
all. Mogens was walking around looking for a place
with some shelter, but the wind seemed to be blowing
on all sides of the church. He threw himself down near
the embankment and took a book out of his pocket,
but his reading came to nothing. Every time a cloud
passed before the sun, he thought it was getting too
cold and contemplated getting up, but then the light
would return and convince him to stay where he was.
A girl came slowly walking along, a greyhound and a

bird dog running playfully ahead. She stopped and
seemed about to sit down, but when she caught sight
of Mogens, she continued on her way across the cemetery and out the gate. Mogens stood up and gazed after
her; she was walking down the highway, the dogs still
frolicking. Then Mogens began to read the inscription
on one of the graves; it soon brought a smile to his
face. Suddenly a shadow fell over the grave and stayed
there. Mogens glanced to the side. A young, suntanned
man was standing there, one hand in his hunting bag,
the other holding a shotgun.

"That one's not bad," he said, nodding at the
inscription.

"No," said Mogens, straightening up.

"Tell me," continued the hunter, glancing around
as if he were looking for something, "you've been here
a few days, and I've been wondering about you but
haven't run into you until now. You wander around
so alone, why haven't you paid us a visit? And what on
earth do you do to pass the time? You're not here on
business, are you?"

"No, I'm here for my own amusement."

"And there's plenty of that to be had here," exclaimed the stranger, laughing. "Don't you hunt?
Wouldn't you like to come along with me? I have to
go down to the inn to get some buckshot anyway, and
while you change, I can go over and yell at the blacksmith. So! Will you come along?"

"Yes, I'd like to."

"Oh, that's right—Thora! Have you seen a girl around here?" He leapt up onto the embankment. "Yes, there she is, she's my cousin; I can't introduce you to her, but come along, let's go after her, we made a wager and now you can be the judge. She was supposed to be in the cemetery with the dogs, and then I was supposed to walk past with my gun and bag without calling or whistling to the dogs, and if they followed me then she would lose; now let's see."

A short time later they caught up with the young lady. The hunter looked straight ahead but couldn't keep from smiling, Mogens greeted her as they walked past. The dogs looked at the hunter with astonishment and growled a little, then they looked up at the woman and barked; she tried to pet them, but they moved indifferently away from her and barked after the hunter; step by step they moved farther and farther away, turned around to look at her, and then suddenly took off after the hunter, becoming completely unruly when they reached him, jumping up on him and darting off in all directions and coming back again.

"You lose," he shouted at her; she nodded with a smile, turned around, and left.

The hunt lasted until late in the afternoon. Mogens and Villiam got on well together, and Mogens had to promise to come up to the manor in the evening; that he did, and he came almost every day after that, although he continued to live at the inn in spite of every hospitable invitation.

It was a time of great agitation for Mogens. At first, Thora's presence revived all his burdensome and sorrowful memories; he would often have to turn away to speak to someone else, or leave the room so that his emotions would not completely overwhelm him. She looked nothing like Kamilla, and yet he heard and saw only Kamilla. Thora was petite, slender and graceful, quick to smile, quick to tears, and easily enthused. If she had a lengthy, serious conversation with someone, it was not to establish a rapport, she seemed rather to disappear into herself; if someone was talking or expounding to her, her face and her whole body would display the deepest confidence, and occasionally a certain anticipation. Villiam and his little sister did not treat her exactly like a friend, though not in the least like a stranger either. Her aunt and uncle, and the farmhands, maids, and farmers of the region: they all courted her, but ever so cautiously, almost fearfully—they behaved toward her rather like the wanderer in the forest who sees close at hand one of those exquisite little songbirds with clear, clever eyes, with quick, lovely movements; he is so over-joyed at this tiny living creature, wants so badly for it to come closer and closer, but does not dare move, hardly takes a breath, so that it will not take fright and fly away.

As Mogens saw Thora more and more often, the memories were less and less frequent, and now he began to see her as she really was. There was a time of peace and happiness when he was with her, quiet longing and quiet melancholy when he did not see her. Later he spoke to her about Kamilla and his past life, and it was almost with amazement that he looked back at himself, and at times it seemed almost incomprehensible that he was the one who had thought, felt, and done all the strange things he told her about.

One evening he and Thora were standing on a barrow mound in the garden, gazing at the sunset. Villiam and his little sister were playing tag around the mound. There were delicate, pale colors by the thousands, and strong, brilliant colors by the hundreds. Mogens turned away from them and looked at the shadowy figure at his side: how insignificant she seemed compared to all this glowing magnificence; he sighed and looked again at the colorful clouds. It was not like an actual thought; it appeared, remote and fleeting, lasted a second, and then vanished, as if his eyes were thinking.

"The trolls at Grønhøj are happy, now that the sun has gone down," said Thora.

"Are they now!"

"Oh yes! Don't you know that trolls love the dark?"

Mogens smiled.

"I see you don't believe in trolls, but you ought to. It's so nice to believe in it all, in the barrow people and the elf maidens. I believe in mermaids too, and in the wood nymph, but pixies! What good are pixies and three-legged headless horses of death? Old Maren gets angry when I say that, because she says no God-fearing person would believe what I believe, that it's something that has nothing to do with human beings; but omens and spirits that haunt the church, they're part of the gospels, she says. What do you think?"

"Me? Oh, I don't know... What exactly do you mean?"

"You're certainly not fond of nature, are you?"

"On the contrary!"

"By nature I don't mean the way you view it from a bench or from the top of a hill with stairs leading up, where it's ceremoniously displayed, but nature every day, always. Are you fond of nature in that way?"

"Yes, of course! Every leaf, every twig, every cast of light and every shadow brings me joy. There is no hill so barren, no peat bog so angular, no road so tedious that I can't fall in love with it for at least a moment."

"But what pleasure can you have from a tree or a bush if you can't envision a living creature inside it, opening and closing the blossoms and smoothing out the leaves? When you see a lake, a clear, deep lake, isn't that why you feel affection for it, because you think to yourself that deep down in the water there are living creatures with their own joys and sorrows, their own peculiar lives with peculiar longings? And what beauty can you see in Bredbjerg Grønhøj, for instance, if you don't imagine that inside it's swarming and buzzing with tiny, tiny figures that sigh when the sun comes up but start dancing and frolicking with their splendid treasures when night falls?"

"How strangely beautiful! And that's what you see?"

"Don't you?"

"I can't explain it, but it's something in the color, in the movement and in the form a thing has, and in the life within it, the juices that rise up in trees and flowers, the sun and the rain that make them grow, and the sand that drifts together into hills, and the rain showers that furrow and cleave the slopes. Oh, it doesn't make any sense at all when *I* try to explain it."

"And is that enough for you?"

"Oh, sometimes it's too much! Far too much! Since there are shapes and colors and movements so delicate and lovely, and beyond all this there's also a mysterious world that lives and rejoices and sighs and yearns, and which can speak and sing about all of it, then you feel so forsaken when you can't get any closer to that world, and life becomes so dull and so oppressive."

"No! No! You mustn't think about your sweet-heart in that way."

"Oh, I'm not thinking about my sweetheart."

Villiam and his sister came up to them and they all went inside together.

One morning several days later Mogens and Thora were strolling in the garden. She wanted to show Mogens the arbor house, that was the one place he had not seen; it was a quite long but not very tall greenhouse, the sun was shimmering and playing across its glass roof. They stepped inside, the air was warm and moist, with a strangely heavy and spicy smell, like fresh soil. The beautiful, undulating leaves and the weighty, bedewed clusters of grapes—pierced, illuminated, and glowing with the rays of the sun—spread out beneath the glass covering in one vast green harmony. Thora stood there gazing happily upward, Mogens was restless and would now and then cast a despairing glance at her, and then look up at the foliage.

"Do you know what?" said Thora happily. "I think that now I'm starting to understand what you said up on the hill the other day about form and color."

"Don't you understand more than that?" asked Mogens quietly and gravely.

"No," she whispered, giving him a quick glance and then lowering her eyes and blushing. "I didn't then."

"Then!" repeated Mogens gently, kneeling down before her. "But what about now, Thora?"

She leaned toward him, gave him her hand, and put the other to her eyes and wept. Mogens pressed her hand to his breast as he stood up; she lifted her head, and he kissed her on the brow. She looked up at him with radiant, tear-filled eyes, smiled, and whispered: "Thank God!"

Mogens stayed one more week; they agreed that the wedding would be held at Midsummer. Then he left, and then came winter with its dark days, long nights, and a snowfall of letters.

ℭ   ℭ   ℭ

Lights in all the windows of the manor house, garlands and flowers above every door, friends and acquaintances in fancy dress crowding together on the great stone staircase, everyone staring off into the twilight—Mogens had just driven away with his bride.

The carriage rumbled and rumbled, the closed windows rattled, Thora sat there looking out one of them at the ditch along the highway, at Blacksmith Hill where there were primroses in the spring, at Bertel Nielsen's great elder bush, at the mill and the miller's geese, at Dalum Slope, which she and Villiam had slid down on sleds not too many years ago, at Dalum Meadow, at the absurdly long shadows of the horses moving over the gravel heaps, the bog pits, and the rye field. She sat there weeping quietly; every so often as she wiped the moisture from the window she would glance over at Mogens. He was sitting bent over, his traveling cloak open, his hat lying on the front seat rocking back and forth, his hands over his face. Imagine everything *he* was thinking about!

It had been a strange day for him, and the leavetaking had practically robbed him of all courage. She had to say goodbye to all her relatives and friends, to an infinite number of places where remembrances and memories were heaped on top of each other, all the way up to the sky—and all this to go away with him. And he was a fine man to take up with, with his past of crudeness and debauchery. Nor was it so certain that this was all in the past, either; he had changed, of course, and even he had a hard time understanding the way he had been, but you could never be completely rid of that sort of thing, it was all still there, and here he had been given this innocent child to protect and care for, thank God! He had gotten himself into the mire up over his head, and he would probably manage to take her down with him. No! No, she must not—no, she would be allowed to live her bright, easy, young girl's life in spite of him. And the carriage rumbled and rumbled, darkness had fallen, through the windowpanes covered with moisture he caught a glimpse now and then of lights from the farms and houses they were driving past. Thora dozed. Toward morning they arrived at their new home, a manor house Mogens had purchased. The horses were steaming in the cold morning air, the sparrows chirped in the great linden trees in the courtyard, and smoke slowly curled up from the chimneys. Smiling, Thora looked at everything with pleasure as Mogens helped her down; but it was no good, she was so sleepy and too tired even to hide the fact. Mogens showed her to her room and then went out to the garden, sat down on a bench and thought that he was looking at the sunrise, but he was nodding too hard to convince even himself. At noon he and Thora met once again, happy and refreshed, and the rounds were made and there were exclamations of amazement and advice was given and decisions taken, and the most foolhardy suggestions were made, which were unanimously proclaimed practical; and how Thora strained to seem clever and interested when the cows were presented to her, and how hard it was not to be too irrationally overjoyed at the little woolly puppy; and Mogens, how *he* talked about drainage and grain prices as he stood there imagining how Thora would look with those red poppies in her hair.

And then in the evening, as they sat in their garden room and the moon outlined the windows so precisely on the floor, what kind of comedy was he playing when he seriously proposed that she ought to retire for the night, actually retire, since she *must* be so weary, while he kept on holding her hand in his. And what was she playing at when she declared that he was hideous and wanted to be rid of her, that he regretted having married at all; and then they made up, of course, and they laughed, and it gradually grew late. At last Thora went to her room, but Mogens remained sitting in the garden room, thoroughly unhappy that she had left, and then he imagined dark fantasies, that she was dead and gone, and he was quite alone in the world and weeping for her, and weep he did; then he grew angry with himself, stomped up and down the floor and tried to be sensible. Love *did* exist, pure and noble, without any vulgar, earthly passion, yes, it did; and if it did not then it would come someday. Yes, passion destroyed everything, and it was so disgusting, so inhuman; how he hated everything in human nature that was not untainted and pure, delicate and fine! He had been cowed, burdened, plagued by all that was powerful and loathsome; it had overwhelmed his eyes and ears and poisoned all his thoughts. He went to his room. He decided to read and picked up a book; he read but could make no sense of it—nothing had happened to her, had it? No, why should it? He was afraid, nevertheless, that something might happen... No, he couldn't stand it; he tiptoed over to her door; no, it was so quiet, so peaceful; if he listened carefully, he thought he could hear her breathing— how his heart pounded, he thought he could hear that too. He went back to his room and his book. He closed his eyes: how clearly he saw her, he could hear her voice, she bent toward him and whispered—how he loved her, loved her, loved her. It sang inside him, as if his thoughts came in rhythms, and he could see everything he was thinking about so clearly! Quietly, quietly she lay there sleeping, with her arm under her head, with her hair loose, with her hair loose, her eyes closed, she was breathing so lightly. The air was shimmering in there, it was red like the glow of roses—like a clumsy satyr imitating the dance of the nymphs, the rough folds of the blanket limned her elegant figure— no, no! He would not think about her, not think about her in that way, not for anything in the world, no, and then it all came back to him again, it was impossible to keep it away, but it had to be banished, banished! And it came and went, came and went, until sleep came and the night went.

As the sun set on the evening of the following day, they were strolling around the garden together. Arm in arm they walked quite slowly and quite silently up one path and down the next, out of the scent of the reseda, through the fragrance of the rose, into the scent of the jasmine; a few moths fluttered past them, a gadwall quacked out in the grain field; the only other sound was from Thora's silk dress.

"How silent we are!" exclaimed Thora.

"And how far we can walk," continued Mogens. "We must have walked five miles by now."

Then they walked on for a while in silence.

"What are you thinking about?" she asked.

"I'm thinking about myself."

"That's just what I'm thinking."

"Are you thinking about yourself too?"

"No, about you, Mogens, about you."

He drew her closer to him. They walked toward the garden room, the door stood open; it was brightly lit inside, and the table with the snow-white cloth, the silver dish of dark red strawberries, the gleaming silver coffeepot and candlesticks made a festive impression.

"It's like in the fairy tale, when Hansel and Gretel come upon the gingerbread house out in the woods," said Thora.

"Do you want to go in?"

"You forget that there's a witch inside who will cook and eat us unfortunate little children. No, it's much better if we resist the sugar windows and gingerbread roof and take each other by the hand and wander out into the black, black forest."

They walked past the garden room. She leaned close to Mogens and continued: "It could also be the palace of the great Turk, and you are the Arab from the desert who wants to abduct me, and the guard is after us; scimitars are flashing and we run and run, but they took away your horse, and so they catch us and stuff us into a big sack, and there we sit, and they drown us in the sea. Let me see, what else could it be…"

"Why can't it just be what it is?"

"Oh, it can, but that's not enough… If only you knew how much I love you, but I'm so unhappy—I don't know what it is—we seem so far apart… no…"

She threw her arms around his neck and kissed him hard and pressed her burning cheek against his: "I don't understand it, but sometimes I almost wish that you would hit me—I know it's childish, and that I'm so happy, so happy, but I'm still so *unhappy*."

She rested her head against his chest and wept, and then, as the tears fell, she began to hum, at first quite softly, but then louder and louder:

With longing,
With longing, I live!

"My dear little wife!" and he lifted her in his arms and carried her inside.

In the morning he stood by her bed. The light shone calm and muted through the drawn curtains, blurring all the contours inside, making all the colors saturated and peaceful. It seemed to Mogens as if the air were rising and falling in little waves at her breast. Her head rested at a slight angle on the pillow, her hair lay across her white forehead, one cheek had a stronger blush to it than the other, now and then her gently curved eyelids fluttered faintly, and the lines of her mouth shifted imperceptibly back and forth between unconscious gravity and slumbering smiles. Mogens stood there for a long time gazing at her, happy and calm; the last of the shadows from his past had vanished. Then he tiptoed out and sat down in the parlor, waiting for her in silence. He had been sitting there for some time when he felt her head on his shoulder and her cheek against his.

They went outside together, into the fresh morning. The sunshine rejoiced across the earth, the dew glittered, early awakened flowers were radiant, the lark sang high up in the sky, the swallows swooped through the air. He and she walked across the green field toward the embankment with the yellowing rye, following the path running through it; she led the way, quite slowly, looking over her shoulder at him, and they talked and laughed. The farther they went down the embankment, the more the grain hid them from view; soon they could no longer be seen.

A Shot in the Fog

The little green parlor at Stavnede had apparently been furnished to serve as a passageway leading to the other wing of rooms. At any rate, the low-backed chairs lined up along the pearl-gray paneling did not invite a lengthy stay. In the middle of the wall hung the antlers of a deer, crowning a light-colored patch whose shape clearly indicated that an oval mirror had once occupied the spot. One of the antlers was holding a lady's wide-brimmed straw hat with long ribbons of celadon green. In the corner to the right stood a fowling gun and a thirsty calla lily, in the other corner was a pile of fishing rods with a pair of gloves tangled up in one of the lines. In the middle of the parlor stood a little round table with a gilded base; a large sheaf of ferns lay on its black marble top.

It was late morning. In a great golden haze the sunlight streamed in through one of the highest windowpanes and gradually settled into the midst of the ferns. Some of them were lush green, but most of them were withered; not dry and curled up, for they still retained their shape, but the green color had given way to a boundless chiaroscuro of yellow and brown, from the palest white gold to the ruddiest reddish-brown.

A man about twenty-five years old was sitting by the window and staring at the rich colors. The door to the next room stood wide open, and inside at the piano sat a tall young woman playing. The piano stood near the open window, and the windowsill was so low that she could look out at the lawn and the road, where a young man wearing a rather too stylish riding costume was busy spurring on a dapple gray. The horseman was her fiancé, Niels Bryde was his name; she was the daughter of the house. The dapple gray outside was hers, and it was her cousin who was sitting in the parlor, the son of her uncle, proprietor Lind of Begtrup, who had died destitute and debt-ridden and about whom not one good word had ever been said while he was alive—nor did he deserve any. Lind of Stavnede had taken his nephew Henning under his wing and paid for his education, though only in part; despite the fact that Henning was intelligent and keenly interested in book learning, he was pulled out of Latin school as soon as he was confirmed and brought home to Stavnede to learn agriculture. Now he was a sort of overseer on the farm, but he had no real authority since old Lind could never resist making his own wishes known.

Henning's position was for the most part quite an uncomfortable one. The farm was in poor condition, and nothing could be done to improve it because they lacked capital. There was no question of keeping up with the times or even with their neighbors. Everything had to continue the way it had for God only knows how long: as much as possible for as little as possible. Thus, in bad years, small parcels of land also had to be sold off to raise some ready cash.

On the whole it was bitterly tedious work for a young man to put his time and effort into; add to this the fact that old Lind was quite testy and intractable, and after he had shown Henning the aforementioned generosity, he felt that he owed the boy no further consideration. When he lost his temper, he did not hesitate to tell Henning what a starving brat he had been when he took him in, and if Lind was truly angry he would even go so far as to utter highly scandalous, though probably quite true, innuendos about his father's behavior.

An unmarried uncle down south in Schleswig who carried on an extensive trade in timber had tried several times to get Henning to move down there, and Henning would have run away from his life at Stavnede long ago if he had not fallen so in love with

the daughter that he could not imagine living anywhere without her. It was not a happy love affair,
however. Agathe liked him well enough; they had
played together as children, for that matter as adults
too. But one day the year before, when he declared his
love for her, she had reacted with both anger and astonishment and had told him that she considered it a
reckless joke, and she hoped he would not give her reason to regard it as some kind of obsessive mania by
ever referring to anything of the sort again.

The fact was that the degrading treatment to
which she saw him constantly subjected—and which
he tolerated, probably because of his love for her—had
actually reduced him in her eyes, so that she viewed
him as belonging to a lower caste than her own, not
lower in station or because he was poor, but lower in
emotion, lower in respect.

Shortly thereafter came her betrothal to Bryde.

How Henning had suffered in the three months since
then! And yet he had stayed; he could not give up the
idea of winning her, he hoped that something would
happen, yes, it was not actually a hope, he fantasized
about strange events that might occur to put an end to
the relationship, but he did not expect his fantasies to
become reality; he needed them as an excuse to stay.

"Agathe!" called the rider from outside, reigning
in his horse next to the open window. "You're not

even watching us, and we were just going through our paces so nicely."

Agathe turned her head toward the window, nodded at him, and said as she continued to play, "But I *am* watching you; you almost fell, over there by the snowberry tree." And she played several quick trills on the high notes.

"Go on! Hup!" And she switched over to a raucous galopade.

But the horseman stayed where he was.

"Well?"

"Tell me, are you going to sit there at the piano all morning?"

"Yes!"

"Well, then I think we'll try it—yes, we can probably make it over to Hagested Farm and back by dinnertime, don't you think?"

"Yes, if you hurry. Goodbye, my chubby Blaze. Goodbye, Niels."

Then he rode off. She closed the window and played on, but soon stopped. It was more fun to play when he was riding outside and acting impatient.

Henning sat there staring after the vanishing horseman. How he hated that man; if only he weren't... and they weren't at all suited to each other; if only they'd have a little quarrel so they'd actually end up showing their true selves to each other...

Agathe came into the green parlor, humming the

theme of the nocturne she had just been playing; she went over to the little table and set about arranging the sheaf of ferns. The sunshine fell directly onto her hands; they were large and white, with a lovely shape. Henning was always enchanted by her beautiful hands, and today the sleeves of her dress were quite wide, so that one plump arm was visible all the way up to the elbow. Those hands were so voluptuous with their luxuriant softness, blinding whiteness, and strong contours; and the delicate, shifting play of the muscles, their lovely movements—there was such a charming rippling motion as she stroked her hair. He had so often felt sorry for them when they were forced to leap and stretch across those stupid piano keys, they weren't suited to that at all, they ought to lie still in the lap of a dark silk dress, adorned with large rings like naked women in a harem.

As she stood there attending to the ferns, a look of nonchalant happiness came over her face and goaded Henning. Why should life be so bright and easy for her, when she had plundered every trace of light from him? What if he frightened her out of this bright calm, what if he shoved a little shadow across her path? She had flung his love into the dust at her feet and trod upon it as if it were a lifeless object, as if it were not a human soul, which, full of longing and sick with joy, writhed and moaned with this love...

"He could be in Borreby by now," he said, looking out the window.

"No, he was going to Hagested Farm," she replied.

"Yes, well, it's not far out of the way."

"What do you mean? It's not on the way at all."

"No, I suppose you're right, it's not. Does he still go there anyway?"

"Where?"

"To Borreby, of course, to visit the forest warden."

"I'm sure I don't know. Why would he go there?"

"Oh, it's probably just rumors. You know they have that beautiful daughter."

"And?"

"Well, dear God! Not all men are monks."

"Are people talking about him?"

"People talk about everyone, but he really ought to be more discreet."

"But what are they saying? What are they saying?"

"Oh, rendezvous and… the usual."

"You're lying, Henning! No one's saying that, you're making it all up."

"Then why are you asking? And what pleasure would I gain from telling people about how happy he's making the Borreby girl?"

She left the ferns lying on the table and went over to him. "I never thought you would stoop so low, Henning," she said.

"Yes, my dear, I can understand that you would be upset, it must be dreadful for you that he can't restrain himself—now, at any rate."

"For shame, Henning! It's vile and ignoble of you, but I don't believe your lies."

"I'm not the one saying these things," he said, casting his eyes down. "*I* haven't seen them kissing each other."

Agathe leaned toward him and slapped his cheek with contempt.

He turned as pale as a corpse and looked up at her with eyes more like those of a sick dog than an affronted man. Agathe hid her face in her hands and walked toward the open door. There she stood for a moment, supporting herself as if she felt faint, then glanced over her shoulder at him and said coldly and calmly: "Henning, I want to tell you that I do *not* regret what I did."

Then she left.

Henning sat there for a long time, benumbed, then stumbled up to his room and threw himself onto his bed. He was disgusted with himself. Now it was all over—the smartest thing for him to do would be to put a bullet in his head; to live, slinking through life with a scowling look like a kicked dog? No! With her blow she had stamped him with the mark of the thrall, and she was right, there was no other way to respond to such baseness. How he had loved her! Feverishly, insanely; but not like a man, like a dog—in the dust at

her feet as if before the image of a goddess. They stood
in the garden, she carved her name into a tree, the
wind played with her hair, he secretly kissed one of
her fluttering locks and was happy for days after-
wards; no, his love had never been marked by manly
courage or intrepid hope, he was a thrall in every way,
in his love, his hope, his hatred.

Why hadn't she believed what he told her, but instead trusted blindly in Niels? He had never lied to
her; it was the first low deed he had ever committed,
and she had seen through it at once! It was because she
had never credited him with anything except what was
shabby and vulgar. She had never understood him, and
for her sake he had endured this long, miserable life at
Stavnede, where each morsel of bread he put into his
mouth was made bitter with reminders that it was a
gift. The thought of it could make him furious. How
he hated himself for his insane patience, his humble
hope. He could murder her for what she had done to
him, and he *would* be avenged, she would repay him
for the long years of degradation, the thousands of
agonizing hours. Revenge for his lost self-respect, revenge for his slavish love and for the slap on his cheek.

So now he cradled himself in dreams of revenge,
as he had before in dreams of love, and he did not
shoot himself, nor did he leave.

꼰   꼰   꼰

One morning two or three days later Henning was standing down in the courtyard with a shotgun and hunting bag. As he stood there, Niels Bryde came riding up, outfitted for hunting as well, and although these two had exceedingly low opinions of one another, their words were friendly, and they pretended to be especially delighted that it had proved so opportune for them to set out together. They headed down to the Shoal, a rather large, low, flat islet covered with heather out toward the mouth of the fjord. In late autumn the Shoal was often visited by seals who frolicked on the low sand banks jutting out from the shore or slept on the big boulders strewn on the beach. And it was these seals they were going to hunt. When they reached the spot, they went off in separate directions along the water. The gray, misty weather had lured many seals in, and the men could hear each other firing regularly. After a while the mist grew thicker, and by noontime the fog lay heavy and dense over the islet and the fjord; it was impossible to distinguish the stones from the seals at a distance of twenty paces.

Henning sat down on the shore and stared into the fog. It was utterly quiet; only a gentle lapping sound from the water and the anxious peeping of a solitary sanderling occasionally emerged from the heavy, oppressive silence.

He was weary of all these thoughts, weary of hoping, weary of hating, sick of dreaming. To sit here perfectly still and stare drowsily straight ahead, to imagine the world as something far off in the distance, something that was over and done with, to sit here perfectly still and let the hours die out one by one, that was peace, that was almost bliss. Then a song rang out through the fog, carefree and jubilant:

> On May day I will lead my bride home,
> A rose blossom in lily-white gown,
> Play, fiddler, play!
> That day the forest will have green on its height,
> And the meadow will have flowers in its bosom.
> And the moon will be so full that night,
> But the sun will dance itself warm.
> The cuckoo will chirp and happiness foretell,
> And finches will whistle and thrushes will swell,
> But sorrow will keep to its home.

It was the clear voice of Niels Bryde. Henning sprang up; hatred struck him like lightning, his eyes burned, he laughed hoarsely, then he raised his shotgun to his cheek.

> But sorrow will keep to its home

resounded again; he aimed toward the sound in the fog, the last words died in the blast—then all was quiet as before.

Henning had to use the smoking weapon to lean on, he held his breath to listen—no, thank God! There was only the lapping of the water and the distant screech of the frightened gulls. Wait! There was a moan from deep in the fog. He threw himself to the ground, pressed his face into the heather, and covered his eyes. Clearly he envisioned the contorted face, the convulsing limbs, and the red blood gushing steadily from his breast, spurt after spurt, driven forth with every beat of his heart—dripping into the brown brush of the heather, trickling down the branches and stems, and then seeping away among the black roots.

He raised his head and listened: he still heard moaning, but he did not dare go over there, no, no! He gnashed his teeth in the heather, burrowed his hands into the loose earth as if seeking a hiding place, thrashed back and forth like a madman, but it still had not finished in the fog; he still heard the moaning.

At last there was silence. He lay for a long time listening, then he crawled slowly on his hands and knees into the fog. It was a long time before he could see anything, then he finally found him at the foot of a small bank of earth. He was stone dead; the shot had struck him right in the solar plexus.

Henning lifted the body in his arms and carried it across the Shoal down to the boat they had come in, then he took up the oars and rowed toward land. From the moment he saw the body, his agitation subsided and a quiet, dull melancholy took its place. He thought about the transitoriness of life and about how he might best break the news to those waiting at home.

When he reached land, he walked up to the farm-house to find some transportation. The man asked him how the accident had happened. The account took shape almost of its own accord on Henning's lips: Bryde had crept across a dune over on the west side with his shotgun in his hand, the trigger at half-cock, of course; something had caught hold of it, and the gun had gone off. Henning could tell by the shot that they were near each other, and he had called to Bryde; when he received no reply, he grew uneasy and walked in the direction of the shot. He found him ly-ing right at the bottom of the earth embankment, but by then he was already dead.

He told the whole story calmly, in a muted, sor-rowful tone of voice, and had no sense of guilt as he spoke; but when they had put the body into the wagon and it sank down into the straw, fell with its head to one side, and hit the bottom of the cart with a slight thud, then Henning almost fainted, and he was quite sick at heart as they drove the corpse by way of Borup to Hagested Farm.

His first thought after he had delivered the body was to run away, and it was only with the greatest ex-ertion of will that he forced himself to stay until the

funeral was over. During that period of waiting there
was an outward feverish disquiet about him, and an
odd trepidation in his thoughts which made them rove
from one thing to another, unable to concentrate on
anything in particular. This restless swirling and cir-
cling which he was helpless to control was about to
drive him mad, and when he was alone he fell into the
habit of counting, or he would hum, keeping time
with his foot, trying in this way to trap his thoughts
and avoid being whirled into their terrifying, exhaust-
ing reel.

Finally the funeral was held.

The following day Henning was on his way to his
uncle, the lumber dealer, to ask him for a position
with his firm. He found his uncle in a greatly de-
pressed state of mind. His old housekeeper had just
died the month before, and a few days ago it had been
necessary for him to fire his manager on grounds of
disloyalty. So Henning was more than welcome. He
enthusiastically threw himself into the business, and
after a year he took over as the director.

଼ଃ   ଼ଃ   ଼ଃ

Four years later, many changes have occurred. The
lumber dealer is dead, and Henning has been named
his primary heir. Old Lind of Stavnede has also gone
to his ancestors, but he left the farm so heavily in debt

that it had to be sold, and after its sale almost nothing is left for Agathe. The new owner of Stavnede is Henning, who has given up the lumber business and returned to agriculture. Niels Bryde has been succeeded at Hagested Farm by a certain Klavsen, who on the first of the month will be married to Agathe, now living at the parsonage. She is more beautiful than ever. Things are different for Henning. You cannot tell by looking at him that he has been successful. He looks almost old. His features are sharper, his gait is listless, he walks slightly bent over, speaks little and more softly; his eyes have acquired a strangely dry sheen, and his gaze has grown restless and wild. When he thinks he is alone, he mutters to himself and gesticulates. This is why people in the region think that he drinks.

But that is not the reason. Day and night, at any time at all, he never feels safe from thoughts about the murder of Niels Bryde. His spirit and his talents have withered because of this perpetual anxiety, for when the thoughts come, they do not appear in the form of regret or gloomy anguish, but as vibrant, flaming horror, a terrifying delirium which distorts his vision so that everything moves, streaming, dripping, oddly trickling, and everything changes color, pale as a corpse or dark red like blood. And there is a suction in all of this streaming, as if all his veins were being drained, all the fine fibers of his nerves sucked out, and

his breast heaves in nameless terror, but no redeeming
scream, no relieving sigh can make its way across his
pale lips.

Such sights are the consequence of his thoughts,
that is why he fears them, that is why his gaze is uneasy and his gait so listless. Fear is what has stripped
his powers; what strength he still possesses resides in
his hatred. For he hates Agathe, hates her because his
soul has been destroyed by his love for her, his life's
joy has been ruined by her, and his peace; but most of
all he hates her because she knows nothing of the
world of agony and wretchedness which she has created; and now when he talks to himself with menacing
gestures, he is thinking of revenge, he is contemplating
plans for revenge. But he does not let on, to Agathe he
is friendliness itself; he pays for her dowry, and later
he escorts her to the altar, and his kindness does not
cool after the wedding. He has helped Klavsen and ad-
vised him in every way, and they jointly undertook
several large speculative enterprises that brought excellent results. Then Henning stopped, but Klavsen
wanted to continue, and Henning promised to support him with advice and assistance. And so he did. He
extended significant sums of money to him, and
Klavsen moved from one speculative negotiation to
another. He won some, but lost many; the more he
speculated, the more zealous he became. Finally, a
quite significant venture was about to make him a rich

man. It required several large advance payments, and
Henning continued to help him; with the last payment still to be made, Henning pulled out. Klavsen
thought the prospects were extremely promising, and
if he withdrew from the transaction at this stage he
would be ruined, but he could not make the payment.
So he signed Henning's name to a couple of promissory notes; no one would suspect, and the profits
would soon follow.

The venture fell through. Klavsen was effectively
ruined. The due date for the notes was at hand; a last
effort had to be made, so he sent Agathe up to
Stavnede. Henning was astonished to see her, because
she had given birth not long before, and the weather
was raw and rainy. He led her into the green parlor,
and she told him about the failed speculation and
about the notes.

Henning shook his head and told her calmly and
gently that she must have misunderstood her husband;
a man did not sign another man's name to promissory
notes, that was a crime, an outright crime that the law
punished with imprisonment.

No, no, she hadn't misunderstood her husband,
she knew it was a crime, that's why he had to help; if
only he wouldn't raise any objection to the signature,
then everything would be fine.

But then he would have to pay the notes, and he
couldn't do that, he had already invested so much

money in Klavsen's undertakings that he was overextended. He could not do it.

She wept and pleaded.

But she had to consider that he had already lost an enormous amount on Klavsen. When she told him the venture had failed it was actually as if someone had boxed his ear, so surprised and bewildered did he feel. Using that expression, it occurred to him that she had struck him once, did she remember that? No?... It was one day when he was teasing her about Bryde... she really couldn't remember? Well, in loving indignation she had slapped him on the cheek, right on this cheek.

Yes, but *couldn't* he help them?

It had been in this very room. Ah, that was a different time, an extraordinary time. He even thought that he had proposed to her once, he seemed to remember that. Imagine if she had accepted him, but it was foolish to talk about that; no, Bryde was a handsome man, and to think he should come to such a sad end, that handsome young man.

Yes, yes, but was there truly no way out, none at all?

She shouldn't believe that story about the notes, it was just something Klavsen had told her to see whether he could still extract a bit more out of him, it was a trick, Klavsen was cunning. Very clever of him, very clever.

No, what she said was really true. If she came
back with a refusal, Klavsen would have to flee to
America, the carriage that was to take him to the train
station in N. had already been brought out when she
left to come here.

He never would have believed this of Klavsen. It
was the basest chicanery! To bring adversity down
upon the one who had helped him again and again. He
must be truly wicked. It was shocking. And then to
bring disgrace upon his wife and his innocent child.
She should hear what people would be saying! Poor
Agathe, poor Agathe!

She threw herself at his feet and implored,
"Henning, Henning, have pity on us!"

"No, a thousand times no, *my* name shall not be
tarnished, I will not help a criminal."

Then she left.

Henning sat down and wrote to the police in N.,
telling them to arrest Klavsen for forgery when he
turned up at the train station. A courier was sent off
with the letter.

That evening he heard that Klavsen had gone; the
next day he was arrested in N.

Agathe had to retire to her bed when she arrived
home; weakened as she was by her recent convales-
cence, she had not been able to bear the exertion and
the strong emotions. The news that Klavsen had been

caught broke her completely. Her illness took on a violent, feverish quality, and three days later word was sent to Stavnede that she was dead.

The day before the funeral Henning went to Hagested Farm. The weather was dark and foggy, the leaves were falling in droves, there was a rank, mouldering smell in the air.

They led him to the death chamber; the windows were covered with white cloth, a couple of candles were burning at the corpse's headboard. The air was heavy with the scent of flowers from the many wreaths and with the smell of the coffin's varnish.

His mood was almost festive at the sight of her lying there in that wondrous white burial gown. They had placed a white linen over her face; he let it lie there. Her hands lay folded on her breast; they had given her white cotton gloves. He took her hand, pulled off the glove, and pressed it to his breast. Then he stared with curiosity at her hand, bending the fingers and breathing on them as if to warm them. For a long time he held her hand in his; it grew darker and darker in the room, the fog grew thicker outside. Then he leaned over her face and whispered, "Farewell, Agathe! I want to tell you before we part that I too do not regret what I have done." Then he let go of her hand and left.

When he came outdoors he could barely see the barn, the fog was so thick. He followed the shoreline home. So he had his revenge—but what now? What about tomorrow, and the day after that? It was so quiet; only a slight sound from the water over there, but he could not hear his heart—oh, yes, it was beating, but so faintly, so faintly. What was that? It sounded like a shot! And another one! He shook his head, smiled and mumbled: "No, not two, only one, only one." He was so weary, but to rest—he had no peace to rest. He stopped for a moment and looked around: there was not much to see, the fog formed a wall around him, fog overhead, fog all around, sand down below; there lay his footprints in the sand in a straight line; they reached as far as the center of the circle of fog, no further; he walked on a bit; no, they reached no further than to the middle, but behind him, where he had been walking, there were circles full of his tracks. But he was so weary; it was the sand that was so hard to walk on—each footstep had cost him some of his strength. Yes! It was a row of graves for his vanished strength—and on the other side, there the sand lay even and smooth and expectant—a shudder raced through him: it's someone walking on my grave, someone is walking in my footsteps, there's a rustling over there in the fog like the sound of a woman's dress, there's something white over there in the white fog. He kept walking as vigorously as he could. His legs were shaking under him, everything went black, but he had to keep going, on through the

fog, because whatever was in there was still following
him. It came closer and closer, his strength was about
to give out, he staggered from side to side, strange
flashes of light shot past his eyes, sharp, piercing
sounds rang in his ears, cold sweat broke out on his
forehead, his lips opened in terror, then he collapsed
onto the sand. And out of the fog it came, shapeless
and yet recognizable, creeping over him, slowly and
heavily. He tried to get up, then it grabbed him by the
throat with clammy white fingers…

The next day, when Agathe was to be buried, the
procession waited for a while, but no one came from
Stavnede to accompany her.

Two Worlds

The Salzach is not a cheerful river, and there is a little village on its eastern bank that is quite dismal, quite poor, and singularly silent.

Like a wretched flock of stunted beggars who have been stopped by the water and have nothing to offer as ferry toll, the houses perch along the very edge of the bank with their palsied shoulders hunched against each other, poling forlornly in the grayish current on their rotted, crutchlike posts as their big dull windowpanes behind the outside galleries stare from beneath the jutting brows of the shingled roofs—stare with a scowl of malignant anguish at the happier houses across the river, scattered individually, or two by two, and here and there in cozy clusters across the green slope far off in the misty golden distance. But there is no glow surrounding the poor houses, only brooding darkness and silence weighted with sounds from the river gliding past,

torpidly yet never ceasing, murmuring to itself on its
way, so weary of life, so strangely oblivious.

ल्ड   ल्ड   ल्ड

The sun was about to go down; the crisp glass hum of
the cicadas began to fill the air on the other side, blown
across now and then by sudden dull gusts of wind that
arose and died away in the growth of thin osiers on the
fringe of the river.

From upriver came a boat.

The frail, emaciated figure of a woman stood in
one of the farthest houses, leaning over the parapet of
the gallery and gazing toward the boat. She shaded her
eyes with her almost transparent hand; up where the
boat was, the sheen of the sun lay golden, glittering
sharply across the water, and the boat seemed to be
sailing on a mirror of gold.

Through the limpid dusk the woman's waxen face
shone as if illuminated from within; it was as distinct
and sharp as the crests of foam that even on the darkest
nights whiten the waves of the sea. Anxiously her hope-
less eyes roved, a curiously wan smile lay on her weary
mouth, but the vertical furrows on her prominent
curved brow spread a shadow across her whole face of
the certainty of despair.

The bells began to toll in the little village church.

She turned away from the glow of the sun, rocking her head back and forth as if to escape the clamor of the bells as she muttered, almost in reply to the incessant ringing: "I cannot wait, I cannot wait."

But the sound went on.

As if tormented she paced the gallery; the shadow of despair had grown even deeper, and she breathed heavily, like someone choked by tears and yet unable to weep.

For years and years she had suffered from a painful illness which gave her no respite, whether she lay down or walked about. She had sought out one wise woman after another, had dragged herself from one holy spring to another, but all in vain. Finally she had joined the September procession to St. Bartholomäus, and there a one-eyed man had counseled her to bind together a whisk of edelweiss and withered rue, of corn smut and cemetery ferns, a lock of her hair and a splinter from a coffin; she should then toss it at a young woman, robust and healthy, who would appear on the rippling water. Then the illness would leave her and be transferred to the other.

She now had the whisk concealed in her bosom, and up on the river a boat appeared, the first one since she had bound together the magic bundle. She stepped up to the parapet of the gallery once more; the boat was so close she could see that there were five or six passengers on board. They seemed to be strangers. In the bow stood the boatman with a sounding pole, at the tiller sat a woman steering, and a man sat next to her, making sure that she steered according to the boatman's signals; the others sat in the middle of the boat.

The sick woman leaned far forward; every feature of her face was tense and searching, and she had her hand at her bosom. Her temples pounded, her breathing almost stopped, and with flaring nostrils, flushed cheeks, and wide-open, rigid eyes she waited for the boat to draw near.

The voices of the travelers were already audible, now clear, now only a muted murmuring.

"Happiness," said one of them, "is a perfectly heathen notion. You won't find the word anywhere in the New Testament."

"Bliss, then?" suggested another inquisitively.

"No, now look here," someone interjected, "the ideal goal of a conversation may well be to digress from the subject, but I think we could accomplish that suitably by returning to the topic we started with."

"Ah yes, the Greeks..."

"First the Phoenicians?"

"What do you know about the Phoenicians?"

"Not a thing! But why do we always have to pass over the Phoenicians?"

The boat was right below the house now, and just as it pulled up, someone on board lit a cigarette. In a few brief flares the light fell on the woman at the tiller, and in the reddish glow a fresh, youthful female face was visible, with a happy smile on her half-open lips and a dreamy expression in her clear eyes gazing up at the dark sky.

The light was extinguished, a little splash was heard, as though something had been tossed into the water, and the boat drifted past.

ᖇ   ᖇ   ᖇ

It was about a year later. The sun was going down between banks of heavy, lumbering clouds that cast a blood-red glow on the river's murky waters; a fresh wind swept down over the plain. There were no cicadas, only the gurgling of the river and the swish of the quivering rushes. In the distance a boat could be seen coming downstream with the current.

The woman from the gallery was down by the bank. When she had thrown her magic bundle after the young girl that day, she fell in a faint up on the gallery, and the strong emotions, perhaps combined with the help of a new doctor who had come to the region, had brought about a change in her illness, and after a difficult transition period she began to get better and a few months later was fully recovered. In the

beginning she was almost intoxicated with this feeling
of health, but it did not last long; she grew despondent
and anxious, restless and despairing, for she was constantly haunted by the vision of that young girl in the
boat. At first the girl appeared to her as she had seen
her, young and blooming, she knelt at her feet and
looked up at her with pleading eyes; later the vision
disappeared, but she knew where it was and that it was
there, for she heard the girl moaning quite softly, in
her bed in the daytime and in a corner of her room at
night. Lately it had fallen silent and had become visible
once more; the image of the girl sat before her, pale
and emaciated, staring at her with unnaturally large,
uncanny eyes.

Tonight she had come down to the river bank; she
had a whittled stick in her hand and was scratching one
cross after another into the soft silt; once in a while she
would straighten up to listen, and then go on drawing.

Then the bells began to toll.

She meticulously finished the cross, put down the
stick, knelt down, and prayed. Then she walked into
the river until it was up to her waist, folded her hands,
and dropped into the grayish-black water. And it took
her, pulled her down into the depths, and glided by as
always, sluggish and sad, past the village, past the fields—
gone.

The boat had now come quite close; on board were
the young people who had once helped each other steer;
now they were on their honeymoon. He sat at the tiller,

she stood in the middle of the boat, draped in a large gray shawl, a little red hood over her head... stood there leaning on the short, sailless mast and humming.

Then they drifted right beneath the house. She nodded with pleasure to the helmsman, looked up toward the sky, and proceeded to sing. She sang, leaning against the mast, with her eyes turned toward the racing clouds:

> *Behind wide moats*
> *Is my nest secure?*
> *Are you built firm, my fortress of joy,*
> *And will the ramparts deflect sorrow and wrath?*
> *But what do I glimpse from the high gallery,*
> *Closing in where sun-red shadows dwell?*
> *I know those shadows...*
> *Out there gathering,*
> *Out there roaming,*
> *Are banished thoughts*
> *From my days of woe.*
>
> *Come in, you shades, come in and guest*
> *My fortress and sit next to my heart*
> *And drink from the goblet shining gold*
> *In the rich, radiant hall of joy.*
> *A toast to happiness ere it came,*
> *A toast to the poverty of hope.*
> *A toast to dreams!*

There Should Have Been Roses

There should have been roses.

Big, pale yellow ones.

And they should have been hanging over the garden wall in a luxuriant cluster, randomly sprinkling their delicate petals into the wheel ruts of the road: an elegant hint of all the lavish floral riches within.

And let them have the subtle, fleeting rose scent, impossible to capture, which seems to come from unknown fruits that the senses rave about in dreams.

Or should they be red, those roses?

Perhaps.

They could be those small, round, robust roses, and they would hang there on slender vines, shiny-leaved, red, and fresh, like a greeting or a kiss blown to the wanderer who, weary and dusty, comes walking down the middle of the road, relieved that he now has only half a mile to Rome.

What might he be thinking? What might his life be like?

Well, now he is hidden by the houses, they hide everything in that direction; they hide each other and the road and the city, but in the other direction there is plenty to see; there the road curves in a languid arc that dips gradually down toward the river, down to the dreary bridge. And beyond that is the vast expanse of the countryside.

The gray and green of such broad plains... the fatigue of many weary miles seems to rise up from them and settle oppressively over a man, making him feel lonely and abandoned, causing him to search and yearn. And so it is much better to settle comfortably in a nook like this one, down between high garden walls, where the air is warm and gentle and still, to sit on the sunny side where a bench nestles into a kind of niche in the wall, to sit here and look at the glistening green acanthus in the ditch by the side of the road, at the silver-flecked thistles and the dull-yellow autumn flowers.

On the long gray wall directly opposite, a wall full of lizard holes and crevices with dried wall grass— that's where the roses should have been, and they should have peeked out of that spot where the long, uniform surface is broken by a great convex basket of wonderful old scrollwork, a wrought-iron basket forming a spacious balcony more than chest high; it must have been refreshing to clamber up there when they grew weary of the enclosed garden.

As they often did.

They hated the magnificent old villa that is said to be inside, with its marble staircases and its coarse-fibered tapestries; and the ancient trees with their proud black crowns, pine and laurel, noble ash, cypress and live oak—the trees have been hated throughout their entire existence with the hatred that restless hearts harbor toward the ordinary, the customary, the uneventful, whatever does not share their yearning and so seems to stand in their way.

But up on the balcony they could at least lose themselves in the view, so there they have stood, one generation after another, all of them gazing out, each with his own mood, his own vista. Gold-banded arms have rested on the edge of this iron balcony, and many a silk-swathed knee has pressed against its black scroll-work while variegated ribbons fluttered from all its balusters as signs of love and promises of rendezvous. Wives, heavy with child, have stood there too and sent impossible messages off into the distance. Women, big, voluptuous and abandoned, pale as hatred... if only death could be dispatched by a thought, if only hell could be opened by a wish!... Women and men! It is always women and men, even those gaunt white virginal souls who, like a flight of doves led astray, press against the black grating and shout: seize us, take us out to fancied noble hawks!

A *commedia* might come to mind here.

The setting would be appropriate for a *commedia*.

The wall over there with the balcony should stay just the way it is; but the road would have to be wider, expanding to a circle, and in the middle there must be a stylish old fountain, built from yellowish tuff with a basin of cracked porphyry; as the fountain's centerpiece, a dolphin with its tail broken off and one nostril plugged. Out of the other spurts a thin stream. On the other side of the fountain is a semicircular bench of tuff and fired stone.

The loose grayish-white dust, the reddish cast stone of the bench, the yellowish, porous hewn tuff, the dark honed porphyry glistening with moisture, and the lively little gleaming silver stream; the materials and colors are well matched.

The characters are two courtiers.

Not from a particular historical period, for real courtiers never actually resembled the ideal. These courtiers are the kind who love and dream in classic literature.

It is only their attire that has something historical about it.

The actress who is to play the younger courtier is dressed in fine silk that fits quite snugly, pale blue shot through with *fleurs-de-lis* of the brightest gold. This is the most distinctive thing about her costume, along with the innumerable pieces of lace, as many as can possibly be attached. Her clothing does not so much hint at a specific century as it accentuates the youthfully full figure, the splendid blonde hair, and the luminous complexion.

She was married, but after only a year and a half she was divorced from her husband and apparently did not treat him at all kindly. That may well be, but it is impossible to envision anyone more innocent. That is to say, not that dainty primal innocence, which certainly has its own appeal; no, this is that *soignée*, fully developed innocence, which no one can mistake and which goes straight to your heart and enchants you with all the power that is granted only to perfection.

The other actress in the *commedia* is the slender, melancholy one. She is unmarried, has no past, absolutely none; no one knows the slightest thing about her, and yet there is something so telling in those delicately drawn, almost gaunt limbs, in her regular features, pale as amber, shadowed as they are by raven-black locks, borne by that chiseled masculine neck; there is something provocative about that smile— contemptuous, yet sick with longing—and something inscrutable about those eyes, whose blackness has a gentleness to its sheen, like the dark petal of the pansy blossom.

Her costume is a muted yellow, cuirass-like, striped with wide pleats, with a high, stiff collar, and with buttons made of topaz. A narrow ruffle emerges at the edge of the collar as well as at the wrists of the close-fitting sleeves. Her breeches are short, wide, and of a dead green color with pale purple slits. Her tights are gray. The blue courtier's tights are dazzling white, of course. Both are wearing berets.

That is how they look.

And now the yellow courtier is standing on the balcony, leaning over the edge, while the blue one sits below on the fountain bench, leaning back comfortably, with both ring-bedecked hands clasped around one knee. With dreamy eyes he stares out across the countryside.

Then he speaks.

"No, there's nothing in the world like women! I can't understand it... there must be some kind of sorcery in the shape in which they're created. For if I merely see them walk past—Isaura, Rosamund, and Donna Lisa and the others—if I see the way a gown wraps around their figure, how it flows as they walk, it's as if my heart were drinking the blood from all my veins, leaving my head empty and without thought, my limbs trembling and without strength, everything—my entire being gathered in one long, quivering, fearful yearning. But what is this? What could it be? It's as though happiness were walking invisible past my door, and I am supposed to grab it and hold on tight, and then it would be so splendidly mine—but I cannot grab it because I cannot see."

Then the other courtier says from the balcony:

"But when you sat at her feet, Lorenzo, and, lost in her thoughts, she forgot why she had summoned you, and you sat in silence and waited, and her lovely face was above you, more distant in the clouds of its dreams than the star is from you in its heaven, and yet so near your gaze that each feature surrendered to your adoration, each beauteous contour, each lily hue of her complexion in its white calm and in its soft, roseate variation—did it not seem to you then, as she sat there, that she belonged to a different world from the one in which you knelt in adoration, that she possessed another world inside, another world around her where her Sunday-clothed thoughts moved toward goals you did not know and where she loved, far removed from you and yours, from your world and everything else, where she dreamed far and yearned far, and there was not the least space in her thoughts that you could conquer, although you burned to sacrifice yourself for her, to give your life and everything if only there might be between you and her a mere glimmer of something less than companionship, far less than belonging to each other."

"Yes, oh yes, you know it is so. But...." At this moment a golden-green lizard runs along the railing of the wrought-iron balcony. It stops and looks around. Its tail switches...

If only there were a stone...

Take heed, my four-legged friend!

No, it's impossible to hit them, they can hear the stone long before it strikes. Still, he did get a fright.

But the courtiers disappeared at once.

She had been sitting there, so charming, the blue courtier, and with perfect innocent longing in her eyes and a portentous nervousness in all her movements as well as in the slight touch of pain at her mouth whenever she spoke, and even more when she listened to the yellow courtier's soft and rather deep voice, which carried the urgent yet caressing words from the balcony down to her with a tone of derision and a tone of compassion.

And yet does it not seem as though they have both reappeared?

They *are* there, and they have played out more of the *commedia* while they were away, continuing to talk about the vague infatuation of youth which can never find peace but restlessly flits through all the lands of intimations and all the heavens of hope, sick with longing to be included in the strong, sincere fervor of one great collective feeling; that is what they have been talking about, the younger courtier with bitter complaint, the older one growing more and more melancholy. And now the older courtier says, the yellow to the blue, that he must not be so impatient for a woman's reciprocated love to capture him and hold him fast.

"No, believe me," he says, "the love you find, bound by two white arms, with a pair of eyes for your intimate heaven and the certain bliss of a pair of lips—it is too close to the earth and the dust, it has exchanged the free eternity of dreams for a happiness that can be measured in hours and that will age within hours; for no matter how constantly it is renewed, still each time it will lose one of the rays that illuminate, in a halo that cannot wither, the eternal youth of dreams. No, you are the happy one!"

"No, *you* are happy!" replies the blue courtier. "I would give the world to be like you."

And the blue courtier stands up and starts walking down the road into the countryside, and the yellow courtier gazes after him with a sorrowful smile and says to himself, "No, *he* is the happy one!"

But far down the road the blue courtier turns around to face the balcony once more and shouts, as he lifts his beret: "No, *you* are happy!"

There should have been roses.

And now a gust of wind ought to come and shake an entire downpour of rose petals from the blossom-laden branches and swirl them after the retreating courtier.

The Plague in Bergamo

Old Bergamo was on the top of a low hill, fenced in behind walls and gates, and the new Bergamo lay at the foot of the hill, exposed to all the winds.

One day the plague broke out down in the new town and spread horribly; many people died, and the rest took flight across the plain to the four corners of the earth. And the citizens in Old Bergamo set fire to the abandoned town to purify the air, but it did no good; people started dying up there too, at first one a day, then five, then ten, and then a score, and many more than that when the plague was at its peak.

But *they* could not flee the way those in the new town had done.

There were some who tried, but they wound up living the life of hunted animals, hiding in ditches and culverts, under hedgerows and in the middle of the green fields. The peasants, to whose farms the first refugees had brought the plague in many places, stoned every strange soul they encountered and chased them off their land, or else struck them down like mad dogs with no mercy or pity, in righteous self-defense, they felt.

They had to stay where they were, those people in Old Bergamo, and day by day the weather grew warmer, and day by day the grip of the fearful infection grew ever more insatiable. The terror swelled to the brink of madness, and it was as if the earth had swallowed up all there had been of order and proper government and sent the worst in its place.

In the very beginning, when the plague first arrived, people came together in unity and harmony, took care to see that the corpses were buried properly and well, and each day made sure that great bonfires were lit in the squares and marketplaces so that the healthful smoke would drift through the streets. Juniper berries and vinegar were distributed to the poor, and, most importantly, people sought out the churches at all hours of the day, singly or in processions; every day they went into God's house with their prayers, and every evening when the sun set all the church bells cried their lament to Heaven from a hundred swaying throats. And fasts were prescribed, and each day the holy relics were set out on the altars.

Finally, one day when they did not know what else to do, with fanfare of trumpets and tubas they proclaimed from the balcony of the town hall that the

Holy Virgin was to be *Podesta* or Mayor of the town, now and forever.

But none of this did any good; nothing did the least bit of good.

And when people realized this and gradually became convinced that Heaven either would not or could not help, not only did they fold their hands in their laps, saying that what will be, will be. No, it was as though Sin had been transformed, from a hidden, insidious scourge into a raging pestilence both evil and visible, which hand in hand with the corporeal epidemic yearned to kill the soul, just as the former yearned to lay their bodies waste—so unbelievable were their actions, so monstrous their callousness. The air was full of blasphemy and ungodliness, of the moans of gluttons and the howls of drunkards, and their wildest night was no blacker with iniquity than were their days.

"Today we feast, for tomorrow we shall die!" It was as if they had set this to music, to be played on multifarious instruments in one eternal hellish concert. Yes, if every sin had not already been invented, then it would have been invented here, for there was no direction in which they did not turn in their folly. The most unnatural vices flourished among them, and even such uncommon sins as necromancy, sorcery, and the invocation of demons were well known to them, because there were many who thought they would receive from the powers of Hell that protection which Heaven had not deigned to grant them.

Every form of helpfulness or sympathy had vanished from their minds, and each person thought only of himself. The sick were viewed as the common enemies of all, and if some poor devil collapsed on the street, exhausted with the initial feverish vertigo of the plague, there was not a door that would open to him, but with spear-prods and stones he was forced to drag himself away from the path of the healthy.

And day by day the plague grew worse; the summer sun burned down onto the town, not a drop of rain fell, not a breath of wind stirred, and from corpses that lay rotting in the buildings and from corpses that were poorly concealed in the earth, a suffocating stench arose which mixed with the stagnant air in the streets and attracted ravens and crows in swarms and in clouds, so that the walls and rooftops were black with them. And all around the town's encircling wall, huge foreign birds from far away perched at intervals, with rapacious beaks and claws curled in anticipation, and they sat and stared with their calm, greedy eyes as though merely waiting for the unhappy town to become one huge pit of carrion.

It was eleven weeks to the day after the plague had broken out, when the tower sentries and other people who were high up on the ramparts caught sight of an odd procession winding from the plain into the streets of the new town, among the smoke-blackened stone walls and the black ash heaps of the wooden hovels. A horde of people! Probably six hundred or more, men and women, old and young, and they were bearing huge black crosses between then and wide banners above their heads, red like fire and blood.

They are singing as they walk, and strange, despairing sounds of lamentation float up through the stagnant, sultry air.

Brown, gray, and black are their robes, but all of them bear a red mark on their breast. As they come closer the mark is seen to be a cross. Because they do keep coming closer. They crowd up along the steep, wall-lined road that leads up to the old town. There is a multitude of white faces, they have scourges in their hands, there is a rain of fire painted on their red banners. And the black crosses sway from one side to the other in the crush.

An odor rises up from the teeming crowd, of sweat, of ashes, of road dust and old church incense. They are no longer singing, nor do they speak; there is only the herd-like, shuffling sound of their naked feet.

Face after face ducks into the darkness of the tower portal, emerging into the light again on the other side, with light-weary faces and eyelids half closed.

Then the song begins again: a *miserere*, and they grip the scourges and quicken their pace, as if to a battle song.

They look as if they have come from a starved-out town—their cheeks are hollowed, their cheekbones jut out, there is no blood in their lips, and they have dark rings under their eyes.

The people of Bergamo have gathered in crowds to stare at them in amazement and alarm. Their red debauched faces contrast with these pale ones; torpid gazes sated with fornication are lowered before these acrimonious, flaming eyes; jeering blasphemers stand gaping at their hymns.

And there is blood on all of their scourges!

People grew oddly distressed at the sight of these strangers.

But it was not long before they shook off this impression. Some of them had recognized a half-mad shoemaker from Brescia among the cross-bearers, and the entire throng became at once ridiculous because of him. But at least it was something new, a diversion from the ordinary, and when the strangers marched off toward the cathedral, everyone followed behind, the way they would have followed a band of acrobats or a trained bear.

But as they were jostled along, they grew bitter; they felt sobered before the solemnity of these people, and they knew full well that these shoemakers and tailors had come here to convert them, to pray for them, and to speak the words they did not want to hear. And there were two gaunt, gray-haired philosophers who had raised ungodliness to a system; they stirred up the crowd and incited the people from the very evil of their hearts, so that with every step they took toward the church, the mood of the mob became more menacing, their outbursts of anger grew wilder, and it would have taken very little for them to place violent hands on these foreign self-flagellating tailors. But then, not a hundred paces from the church portal, a hostelry opened its doors and an entire flock of drunkards tumbled out, one right on the heels of the other, and they moved to the head of the procession and led the way, singing and bellowing with the most ridiculous gestures of devotion—except for one of them, who turned cartwheels all the way up the church steps, which were overgrown with grass. Then everyone laughed, of course, and they all entered the sanctuary peacefully.

It was strange to be inside again, to stride through that vast, cool room, in the air that was rank with old smoke from snuffed wax tapers, across those sunken flagstones which their feet knew so well, across those stones whose worn decorations and shiny inscriptions had so often wearied their thoughts. And now as their eyes, half out of curiosity, half involuntarily, were drawn to rest in the soft dimness beneath the vaulted ceiling, or slid across the muted confusion of dusty gold and smoke-dimmed colors, or happened to get lost in the singular shadows at the corners of the altar, a kind of longing arose that could not be suppressed.

In the meantime, the men from the hostelry continued their ruckus up by the main altar itself. Among them was a big, powerful butcher, a young man who had taken off his white apron and tied it around his neck so that it hung down his back like a cloak, and in this fashion he celebrated mass up there using the wildest, craziest words, full of obscenities and blasphemy. There was also a pudgy little old man, nimble and quick even though he was so fat, with a face like a flayed pumpkin; he was the parish clerk and responded with all the bawdiest ballads current in the land, and he knelt and curtsied and turned his backside to the altar and rang the bell as if it were a jester's bell and twirled the censer around him; and the other drunkards stretched out full length along the altar rail, roaring with laughter, hiccuping with drink.

And the entire church laughed and howled and gloated at the strangers, and shouted at them to pay close attention so they might discover how Our Lord was regarded here in Old Bergamo. It was not because they had anything against God that they cheered at the pranks, but because they rejoiced at what a thorn this blasphemy must be in the hearts of these holy ones.

The holy ones stopped in the middle of the nave, and they moaned in agony, their hearts boiling with hatred and thirsting for revenge, and with their eyes and hands they prayed to God to avenge Himself for all this scorn displayed to Him in His own house. They would gladly perish along with these blasphemers if only He would show His power; they would joyfully be crushed beneath His heel if only He would triumph, so that terror and despair and remorse that came too late would scream forth from all these ungodly mouths.

And they began to intone a *miserere,* whose every note resounded like a shout for the rain of fire that came down on Sodom, and for the power of Samson when he toppled the pillars of the house of the Philistines. They prayed in song and in words, they bared their shoulders and prayed with their scourges. Then they knelt, row upon row, bare to their belts, lashing the stinging knots of rope against their welt-covered backs. Frenzied and enraged, they whipped themselves so that the blood sprayed from the whistling scourges. Every blow was a sacrifice to God. If only they could strike harder, so that they might shred themselves into a thousand bloody pieces here in His sight! This body, with which they had sinned against His commandments, must be punished, tortured, reduced to nothing, that He might see how much they hated it, that He might see what curs they were to appease Him, baser than curs beneath His will, the lowest vermin, who ate the dust beneath the soles of His feet! And blow followed blow, until their arms dropped or cramps tied them in knots. There they lay, row upon row, their eyes glittering with madness, foam frothing at their mouths, and blood trickling down their flesh.

And those who witnessed this suddenly felt their hearts pounding, noticed the heat rising in their cheeks, and had difficulty breathing. Something cold seemed to tighten around their scalps, and their knees felt so weak. For they were seized by it; there was a tiny spot of insanity in their brains that understood this madness.

To feel oneself the thrall of the mighty, harsh God, to kick oneself over to His feet, to belong to Him, not in silent piety, not in the passivity of gentle prayers, but to belong to Him in a rage, in the ecstasy of self-abasement, with blood and howls and under the wet, glistening tongues of the scourge. They were disposed to understand; even the butcher fell silent, and the toothless philosophers bowed their gray heads before the eyes they saw all around them.

And it grew quite still inside the church; only a quiet ripple passed through the crowd.

Then one of the strangers, a young monk, stood up and spoke. He was white as a sheet, his black eyes glowed like embers about to be extinguished, and the dark, pain-hardened lines around his mouth looked as if they had been carved out of wood with a knife and were not the creases in a human face.

He stretched up his thin, pain-wracked hands toward Heaven in prayer, and the black sleeves of his
cowl slipped down around his emaciated white arms.

Then he spoke.

He talked about Hell, about the fact that it was
infinite the way Heaven is infinite, about the lonely
world of pain that every one of the damned must en-
dure, filling it with his screams; there were lakes of
sulfur, fields of scorpions, flames that would wrap
around him like a cloak, and silent tempered flames
that would bore their way into him like the blade of a
spear turning in a wound.

It was absolutely still; breathlessly they listened to
his words, for he spoke as if he had seen it with his
own eyes, and they asked themselves: Is he not one of
the condemned who has been sent up from the maw
of Hell to testify before us?

He preached for a long time about the Law and
the severity of the Law: that every syllable of it must
be obeyed, and that any transgression of which they
were guilty would be charged to them, down to the
last lot and the last ounce. "But Christ died for our
sins, you say, so we are no longer bound under the
Law. But I say to you, that Hell shall not be cheated
of a single one of you, and not one of the iron teeth
of Hell's martyr wheel shall be robbed of your flesh.
You believe in the cross of Golgotha? Come. Come!

Come and look at it! I will lead you straight to the foot
of the cross. It was on a Friday, as you know, that they
shoved him out through one of their portals and
placed the heavy end of a cross on his shoulders and
made him carry it to a desolate, barren clay embankment outside the town, and they followed in throngs
and stirred up the dust with their feet so that a red
cloud hung over the place. And they tore the clothes
off him and exposed his body, just as the lords of the
Law command that a criminal be exposed for all to see,
that everyone might see the flesh that is to be committed to torment, and they flung him down onto his
cross and stretched him out on it and pounded a nail of
iron through each of his struggling hands and a nail
through his crossed feet; with clubs they pounded in
the nails, all the way in. And they raised the cross in a
hole in the ground, but it refused to stand straight and
steady, so they rocked it back and forth and drove
wedges and pegs in around it, and those who did this
turned down the brims of their hats so that the blood
from his hands would not drip into their eyes. And
from up there he looked down on the soldiers gam-
bling over his seamless robe and at the whole jeering
mob for whom he was suffering that they might be
saved, and there was not a single sympathetic eye in
the entire throng. And those down below returned the
gaze of the one who hung there, suffering and weak,
they looked at the board above his head on which was
written 'King of the Jews,' and they derided him and

called up to him: 'You who would tear down the temple and build it up in three days, save yourself now; if you are the son of God, climb down from that cross.' Then God's high-born son grew angry and saw that they were not worth saving, those masses that filled the earth, and he ripped his feet off the head of the nail, and he clenched his hands around the nail heads and yanked them out so that the arms of the cross curved like a bow, and he leapt down to earth and snatched up his robe so the dice rattled down the slope of Golgotha, and he slung it around him with the fury of a king and rose up to Heaven. And the cross stood there empty and the great work of atonement was never completed. There is no mediator between God and ourselves; there is no Jesus dead on the cross for us, there is no Jesus dead on the cross for us, *there is no Jesus dead on the cross for us.*"

He was silent.

With his last words he had leaned forward over the crowd, and with his lips and his hands he seemed to cast his testimony down over their heads, and a gasp of terror ran through the church, and in the corners they began to sob.

Then the butcher pressed forward, pale as a corpse, his hands raised and threatening, and he shouted: "Monk, monk, do you want to nail him to the cross again? Is that what you want?" And behind him sounded a hoarse hissing: "Yes, yes, crucify him, crucify him!" And from every mouth it resounded, menacing, imploring, in a storm of shouts up toward the vaulted ceiling: "Crucify him, crucify him."

And clear and bright came a single trembling voice: "Crucify him!"

But the monk looked down over that flutter of outstretched hands, at those contorted faces with the dark openings of the shouting mouths, where the rows of teeth shone white like the teeth of baited beasts of prey, and he spread out his arms toward Heaven in a moment of ecstasy and laughed. Then he climbed down, and his people raised their fiery-rain banners and their empty black crosses and surged out of the church, and once again they passed over the square, singing, and once again through the mouth of the tower portal.

And the people of Old Bergamo stared after them as they trudged down the mountain. The steep, wall-lined road was hazy with light from the sun, which was setting far out across the plain, and just at this moment the crowd was only partially visible because of all that light, but on the red wall surrounding the town the shadows of their great crosses were etched black and sharp, swinging from side to side in the throng.

The song grew more distant; one or two banners still glinted red from the singed black emptiness of the new town; then they vanished across the bright plain.

Fru Fønss

In the charming park behind the old Palace of the Popes in Avignon there is a bench with a view looking out over the Rhône River, across the flower beds of the Durance, over hills and fields, and down onto a section of the town.

One October afternoon two Danish ladies were sitting on this bench: the widow Fønss and her daughter Ellinor.

Although they had been there for several days and were already all too familiar with the view that lay before them, they sat there astonished that this was how things looked in Provence.

Imagine, this was actually Provence! A muddy river with crusts of sandy silt and endless banks of stony-gray pebbles; then pale brown fields without a blade of grass, pale brown slopes, pale brown heights, and light dusty roads; and here and there among the

white buildings groups of black trees, pitch-black
shrubs and trees. Above all this a pallid sky shimmering
with light that made everything even paler, even drier,
and exhaustingly bright; not one glimpse of lush, sati-
ated hues—nothing but starved, sun-tormented colors,
and not a sound in the air, not a scythe cutting through
the grass, not a carriage clattering along the roads. And
the town stretching in both directions, seemingly con-
structed out of silence with all its noontime-quiet
streets, all its deaf-mute buildings with every shutter,
every blind closed—closed, every one of them; buildings that could neither hear nor see.

This lifeless uniformity prompted only a faint
smile of resignation from Fru Fønss, but it made
Ellinor visibly nervous, not ebulliently, anxiously
nervous, but whimpering and listless, the way you
sometimes feel about a day-long rainstorm when all
your sad thoughts rain down as well; or about the idi-
otically comforting ticking of a parlor clock when you
are sitting there incurably disgusted with yourself; or
about the flowers of your wallpaper when, against
your will, the same series of shabby dreams reels
around in your brain, and they are joined together and
broken apart and again conjoined in one nauseating
infinity. This landscape literally had a physical effect
on her, causing her almost to faint, so closely had it
conspired today with memories of a hope that had
been crushed and of deliciously sweet dreams that

were now merely languishing and cloying, dreams which she blushed with shame to remember and yet could never forget. But what did it have to do with this region? The blow had struck her far away from here, in familiar surroundings, by the iridescent Sound, beneath bright green beech trees, and yet here each pale brown rolling hill had this on its lips, and every green-shuttered building stood and kept silent about it.

What had befallen her was the old misfortune of a young heart: she had fallen in love with a man and believed in love again, and then he had suddenly chosen another. Why? For what reason? What had she ever done to him? How had she changed? Wasn't she the same as before? All those eternal questions over and over. She had not said a word to her mother, but her mother had understood every little thing and had been so solicitous toward her; she could have screamed at this solicitude, which knew and yet was not supposed to know, and her mother had understood this too, and so they had gone abroad.

The purpose of the entire trip was to make *her* forget.

Fru Fønss did not have to embarrass her daughter by looking at her face to know where her thoughts were; she simply had to keep an eye on the nervous little hand resting at her side, stretched out with such impotent despair on the slats of the bench, changing its position every second the way someone with a fever

constantly shifts in the hot bed; all she had to do was
to look at this hand to know how weary with life
those young eyes were, staring into the distance, how
the delicate face quivered in torment with each breath,
how pale it was with its suffering, and how sickly the
veins shone blue beneath the sheer skin of her temples.

She felt so sorry for her little girl, and she wanted
so much to have Ellinor leaning against her breast so
that she could breathe over her all the words of solace
she knew; but she held the belief that there are sorrows which should die in secret and should not be
allowed to scream forth in words, not even between
mother and daughter, so that one day under new circumstances, when everything is building up to happiness and delight, those words will not be there as an
obstacle, something that weighs down and enslaves
because the one who uttered them will hear them still
whispering in the other's mind, and imagine them being inspected and turned over and over in the other's
thoughts.

There was also the fact that she was afraid of hurt-
ing her daughter by making it easy for her to confide.
She did not want Ellinor to be ashamed; no matter
how it might ease things, she did not want to help her
over the humiliation that comes from laying open
the most secret corners of one's soul to the eyes of
another. On the contrary, no matter how much more
difficult it made things for both of them, she was glad

to find the same nobility of soul which she herself possessed present in a certain healthy reticence in her young daughter.

Once—once upon a time, many many years ago when she herself was an eighteen-year-old girl, she had loved with all her soul, with every sense in her body, every hope, every thought. But it was not to be, it could not be; he had had nothing but his faithfulness to offer, to be tested throughout an endless betrothal. And there had been circumstances in her family that could not wait. So she had taken the man they gave her, the one who was master of these circumstances. They were married and then came the children: Tage, her son who was here in Avignon with them; her daughter who was sitting by her side, and it had all turned out better than she could have expected, both brighter and easier. Eight years it lasted, and then her husband died, and she mourned him with a sincere heart, for she had grown fond of that delicate, thin-blooded soul who, with a tense and egotistical ardor, had an almost morbid love for whatever had to do with family and kinship, and who, in the whole great world outside, cared for nothing but what the world thought, only its opinion, nothing more. After her husband's death she had lived mainly for her children but had not shut herself up with them; she took part in the social life that was natural for a young and well-to-do widow, and now her son was twenty-one years

old, and she had only a few days left before she turned
forty. But she was still beautiful; there was not a touch
of gray in her heavy, dark-blonde hair, not a wrinkle
around her large, lively eyes, and her figure was slim in
its well-formed fullness. Her strong, delicately etched
features were emphasized by the darker, more in-
tensely hued complexion which the years had brought
her, but there was a sweetness in the smile around her
full, sculpted lips, an almost propitious youthfulness
in the softly bedewed sparkle of her brown eyes which
made everything calm again and tender. And yet there
was the great roundness of her cheek, the strong-
willed chin of a mature woman.

"I think Tage is coming," said Fru Fønss to her
daughter when she heard laughter and several shouts
in Danish on the other side of the thick hedgerow of
hornbeam trees.

Ellinor pulled herself together.

And here came Tage—Tage and the Kastagers,
Merchant Kastager from Copenhagen with his sister
and daughter; Fru Kastager was ill in bed back at the
hotel.

Fru Fønss and Ellinor made room for the two
ladies; for a moment the gentlemen made an attempt
to converse standing, but they were soon enticed by
the low graystone wall surrounding the viewpoint,
and there they sat, saying only the most essential
things, for the newly arrived party was tired from a
day trip on the train out into rosy-blushing Provence.

"Hey!" shouted Tage, slapping the palm of his hand on his light-colored pants. "Look at that!"

They all looked.

Out in the brown landscape a dust cloud appeared, above it a dusty cape, and in between there was a glimpse of a horse. "It's that Englishman I told you about, who arrived the other day," said Tage to his mother. "Have you ever seen anyone ride like that?" He turned to Kastager. "He reminds me of a gaucho."

"Mazeppa?" Kastager inquired.

The rider vanished.

Then they stood up and set off for the hotel.

They had met these Kastagers in Belfort, and since they were taking the same route down through southern France and along the Riviera, they had been traveling together for a while. Here in Avignon both families had stopped; the merchant's family because his wife was having trouble with a varicose vein, and the Fønsses because Ellinor apparently needed to rest.

Tage was delighted with this companionship because day by day he was falling more and more incurably in love with the lovely Ida Kastager; but Fru Fønss was not as pleased, for although Tage was quite confident and mature for his age, there was no need for haste with any betrothal, and especially with the little Kastager. Ida was a splendid girl, Fru Kastager was a very cultured lady from an excellent family, and the merchant himself was clever, rich, and respectable, but there was an aura of ludicrousness about him, and a

smile would appear on people's lips or a wink would
come to their eye whenever Merchant Kastager was
mentioned. He was so ardent and so extraordinarily
enthusiastic, so ingenuous, so noisy and so convivial—
that was precisely the reason, because so much discre-
tion is required to be around an enthusiastic person.
But Fru Fønss did not like to think about Tage's
father-in-law being mentioned with a wink of an eye
and a smile on the lips, and so she remained somewhat
cool toward the family, to the great sorrow of love-
struck Tage.

The morning of the following day, Tage and his
mother took a walk to see the little museum in town.
They found the gate open, but the doors to the collection were closed; ringing the bell proved fruitless. But
the gate opened onto the rather small courtyard,
which was surrounded by a newly whitewashed arcade
whose short, thick-waisted pillars were reinforced
with black iron braces.

They walked around looking at what was displayed along the walls: Roman cenotaphs, fragments
of sarcophagi, a headless draped figure, two vertebrae
from a whale, and a number of architectural motifs.

On all of the curiosities there were fresh traces of
the mason's whitewash brush.

Then they were back at their starting point.

Tage ran up the stairs to see whether there might

be someone in the building, and Fru Fønss began to stroll back and forth in the arcade.

As she was on her way back to the gate, a tall bearded gentleman with a suntanned face appeared at the end of the passageway, right in front of her. He had a guidebook in his hand; he turned his head to listen and then looked straight at her.

She thought at once of the Englishman from the day before.

"Pardon me, madam," he began hesitantly, greeting her.

"I am a foreigner," replied Fru Fønss. "No one seems to be home, but my son ran upstairs to see...."

These words were exchanged in French.

At that moment Tage appeared. "I've been everywhere," he said, "even inside an apartment, but there wasn't a soul."

"I hear," said the Englishman, this time in Danish, "that I have the pleasure of being in the company of countrymen."

He greeted them again and took a few steps back, as if to imply that he had merely said this so they would know that he could understand what they said; but suddenly he stepped closer and, with a tense, emotional expression on his face, said: "It's not possible that madam and I are old acquaintances, is it?"

"You're not Emil Thorbrøgger, are you?" Fru Fønss exclaimed, stretching out her hand.

He grasped it. "Yes, it's me," he said joyfully, "and it's you!"

He practically had tears in his eyes as he gazed at her.

Fru Fønss introduced her son Tage.

Tage had never in his life heard mention of this Thorbrøgger, but that was not what he was thinking; rather that the gaucho had turned out to be a Dane, and in the ensuing pause, when someone had to say something, he could not help exclaiming: "And here I said yesterday that you reminded me of a gaucho!"

Well, that was rather close to the truth too, said Thorbrøgger, since for twenty-one years he had lived on the plains of La Plata and in all those years he had probably spent more time on horseback than on foot.

And now he had come here to Europe.

Yes, now he had sold his land and his sheep and had come to take a look around in this old world where he belonged; but he was ashamed to say that he frequently found it quite boring, this traveling for his own pleasure.

Perhaps he was homesick for the prairies?

No, he had never felt any longing for places or countries; he thought he simply missed his daily work.

They conversed in this way for a while. Finally the caretaker arrived, red-faced and out of breath, with heads of lettuce under his arm and a bunch of fiery-red tomatoes in his hand, and they were admitted into the

stuffy little art collection, where they gained only the
vaguest impression of the yellowish stormy skies and
black waters of Vernet the Elder; on the other hand
they became quite well acquainted with each other's
life and destiny during the many years that had passed
since they parted.

For he was the one she had loved that time when
she was promised to another; and during the following
days, as they spent much time together and the others
left them alone, sensing that such old friends must
have a good deal to talk about—during those days they
both soon realized that no matter how much they had
changed during the passing years, their hearts had forgotten nothing.

Perhaps he was the first to feel it, for all the uncer-
tainty of youth, its sentimentality and its elegiac
yearnings, came over him all at once, and it made
him suffer. The mature man disliked suddenly being
robbed of his life's serenity, the self-confidence he
had acquired with time, and he wanted his love to
be of a different character, to be more worthy, more
dignified.

She did not feel any younger, she thought, but it
seemed to her that in her soul a stanched, dammed-up
outpouring of tears had broken open again and had
begun to flow once more. It was such a relief and joy
to weep, and these tears gave her a feeling of richness,
as if she were more worthy and everything in turn

seemed worth more to her; ultimately, a feeling of
youthfulness.

During the evening on one of these days Fru
Fønss was in her room alone; Ellinor had retired early,
and Tage had gone to the theater with the Kastagers.
She had been sitting there in the drab hotel room,
dreaming in the dim light produced by a couple of
candles until her dreams had flagged because of their
constant coming and going, and she grew weary, but
it was the gentle, smiling weariness that spreads over
someone when happy thoughts are about to doze off
in one's mind.

She could not remain sitting there, staring off into
space without so much as a book, and it would be at
least another hour before the theater was out; so she
proceeded to pace up and down the floor, stopping in
front of the mirror to fix her hair.

Of course, she could go down to the reading room
and look at the magazines. No one was ever there at
this hour.

She threw a large black lace veil over her hair and
went downstairs.

Yes, it was empty.

The little room, crowded with furniture, was bril-
liantly lit by half a dozen large gas lamps; it was hot in
there and the air was almost scorchingly dry.

She pulled the veil down around her shoulders.

The white newspapers on the table, the magazine
binders with their big gold letters, the empty plush

chairs, the regular rectangles of the carpet, and the evenly cast folds of the corded drapes—they all looked so mute in that sharp light.

She was still dreaming; she stood there dreaming and listening to the drawn-out singing of the gas jets.

The heat made her feel almost faint.

Slowly, to support herself, she reached up for a big, heavy bronze vase that had been placed on a wall bracket and clutched at its flower-studded rim.

It was pleasant standing there in that way, and the bronze was delightfully cool against her hand. But as she stood there, something else occurred. She began to feel that it was gratifying for her limbs, for her body— this beautifully modeled pose into which she had slipped, and the consciousness of how well it suited her, of the beauty that had come over her at that moment, and even the bodily sensation of harmony, all joined in a feeling of triumph, coursing through her like some mysterious, festive jubilation.

She felt so strong at that moment; life lay before her like a great, shining day, and no longer like a day tilting toward twilight's silent, mournful hours, but like a great, alert span of time, with hot pulses throbbing in each second, with the desire of light, with action and speed and an infinity both inside and out. And she thrilled at the fullness of life and yearned for it with the dizziness and fervor of wanderlust.

She stood like this for a long time, enchanted by her thoughts, forgetting everything around her. Then

suddenly she seemed to hear the silence in the room,
the drawn-out singing of the gas jets, and she let her
hand drop from the vase, sat down at the table, and
began to leaf through a magazine.

She heard footsteps going past the door, heard
them turn around, and then saw Thorbrøgger step
into the room.

A few words were exchanged, but since she
seemed preoccupied with her pictures, he too set
about looking at the journals lying there. They interested him very little, however, for when she glanced
up a moment later, she met his eyes directed at her
with a searching gaze.

He looked as if he were just about to speak, and
there was a nervous, determined expression about his
mouth which told her so clearly what the words
would be that she blushed, and instinctually, as if to
hold the words back, she handed her magazine across
the table to him and pointed at a drawing of some
pampas horsemen slinging their lassos at wild bulls.

He was almost tempted to tell a joke about the
illustrator's naïve ideas about the art of throwing a
lasso; it would be so enticingly easy to talk about that,
compared to what was on his mind, but then he reso-
lutely pushed the magazine aside, leaned slightly over
the table, and said, "I have thought so much about you
since we met. I have always thought so much about
you, both back in Denmark and where I've been living

since. And I have always loved you; sometimes I think that I never loved you until now that we've met again, but I know it's not true, because my love is so great— I have always loved you, I have loved you always. And if I were now allowed to have you for my own, you could not conceive what that would mean to me, if you, taken from me for so many years, if you would come back to me."

He was silent for a moment, then he stood up and drew closer to her.

"Oh, but please say something, I'm standing here talking rashly, I have to talk to you as if to a translator, a stranger, who must repeat my words to that heart I am speaking to, I don't know... please consider my words... I don't know how far or how near, I don't dare express the adoration that fills me... or do I?"

He sank down into a chair at her side.

"Dare I—shouldn't I be afraid that... can it be true? Oh, God bless you, Paula!"

"Nothing will separate us ever again," she said with her hand in his. "Whatever happens, I have the right to be happy at least once, to live fully according to my nature for once, to live out my longings and my dreams. I have never resigned myself; though happiness did not come to me, I never could believe that life was merely tedium and duty; I knew that happy people did exist."

Silently he kissed her hand.

"I know," she said sadly, "that those who judge me most kindly will not begrudge me the joy I feel at knowing myself beloved by you, but they will also say that this should be enough for me."

"But that would never be enough for *me*, and it would never be right for you to let me go like that."

"No," she said, "no."

A little later she went up to Ellinor.

Ellinor was asleep.

Fru Fønss sat down by her bed and looked at the pale child whose features were only barely visible in the scant yellow light of the night lamp.

For Ellinor's sake they would have to wait. In a few days they would part with Thorbrøgger and leave for Nice and stay there alone; all winter long she would live to make Ellinor well. But tomorrow she would have to tell the children what had happened and what was to come. However they might take it, she would be unable to live with them day in and day out, practically closed off from them by such a secret. And they would also need time to get used to the idea; for it would certainly lead to an estrangement between them, great or small depending on the children themselves. As far as the arrangement of their lives was concerned, in relation to her and to him, that would be their decision entirely. She would demand nothing. They were the ones who would have to give.

She heard Tage's footsteps in the parlor and went in to him.

He looked at once so radiant and so nervous that Fru Fønss suddenly thought that something had happened, and she had an idea what it might be.

But he, seeking some sort of prelude to what was in his heart, sat there talking distractedly about the theater, and it was not until his mother went over to him and placed her hand on his brow, forcing him to look up, that he managed to tell her that he had proposed to Ida Kastager and she had said yes.

They talked about this at length, but the entire time Fru Fønss felt that everything she said had a certain coolness to it which she could not overcome; she feared empathizing with Tage too much because of the emotional state she was in, and she would not be able to bear it if her suspicious thoughts conjured up traces of even the faintest shadow of a connection between her acquiescence this evening and her announcement the following day.

Tage, however, was unaware of any coolness.

Fru Fønss did not get much sleep that night, she had far too many thoughts keeping her awake. She thought about how strange it was that he and she should meet, and that when they met they should be as fond of each other as they had been in the old days.

And those *were* the old days, especially for her; she was no longer young, could no longer be young in any case. And that would become apparent, he would have to bear with her, become accustomed to the fact that it was a long time ago that she was eighteen years

young. But she felt young, and she *was* in many re-
spects, and yet she was indisputably aware of her age.
She envisioned it so clearly: in thousands of movements, in her mannerisms and demeanor, in the way
she moved in response to a gesture, the way she smiled
at a reply, ten times a day she would reveal her age
because she lacked the courage to be outwardly as
young as she felt in her soul.

Thoughts came and went, but through it all the
same question constantly arose: about her children
and what they would say.

It was late in the morning of the following day
when she sought their response.

They were sitting in the parlor.

She said that she had something important to tell
them, something that would mean a great change for
all of them, something that would come as a great surprise. She asked them to hear her out as calmly as they
could and not let first impressions carry them away
into inconsiderate actions, for they must know this:
what she was going to tell them had been firmly decided, and nothing they could say would make her
change her mind.

"I am going to remarry," she said, and she told
them how she had loved Thorbrøgger before she
knew their father, how she had been parted from him,
and how they had now found each other again.

Ellinor wept, but Tage jumped to his feet, completely bewildered; then he went over to his mother, knelt down before her, and grabbed her hand, sobbing and choked with emotion, and pressed it against his cheek with indescribable tenderness, an expression of perplexity in every feature of his face.

"But Mother, dearest Mother! What have we done to you, haven't we always loved you? When we were with you and when we were apart, haven't we longed for you as the best that we possessed in all the world? Father we have known only through you; you are the one who taught us to love him, and the fact that Ellinor and I are so fond of each other... isn't that because day after day you have tirelessly shown us what was worthy of love in the other, and hasn't this been true of every person we have grown attached to, haven't we received everything from you? All that we have comes from you, and we worship you, Mother, if only you knew... oh, you have no idea how often our love for you yearns to overflow all boundaries and banks, rising toward you, but you are also the one who has taught us to hold it down, and we never dare come as intimately close to you as we wish we could. And now you say you're going to leave us behind, simply push us aside! But this is impossible. If someone meant to do us the most harm in the world, it could not be as terrible as this. And you don't mean us the most harm in the world, you mean us well, so how can this be possible? Hurry and tell us this isn't true, say: It isn't true, Tage, it isn't true, Ellinor."

"Tage, Tage, pull yourself together and don't make it so difficult for yourself and the rest of us."

Tage stood up.

"Difficult!" he said. "Difficult, difficult, oh, if only it were no more than difficult, but this is terrible—unnatural. It's enough to drive me mad just thinking about it. Do you have any idea what you've made me start thinking of? My mother surrendering to the caresses of a strange man, my mother desired, embraced, and returning the embrace, oh, these are thoughts for a son, thoughts worse than the worst indignity—but this is impossible, it *must* be impossible, it *must* be, for shouldn't there be enough power in a son's prayers? Ellinor, don't sit there crying, come and help me beg Mother to take pity on us."

Fru Fønss held up her hand in protest and said, "Leave Ellinor alone, she's tired enough already, and besides, I told you that nothing can be changed."

"I wish I were dead," said Ellinor, "but everything Tage said is true, Mother, and it's not fair for you, considering our ages, to give us a stepfather."

"Stepfather!" shouted Tage. "I hope he doesn't think for one moment.... You're mad. If he comes in, we will leave; there's no power on earth that could make me tolerate the slightest contact with that man.

It's up to Mother to choose: *him* or *us*! If the newly-
weds go to Denmark, *we* will be exiles. If they stay
here, we must go."

"Is that your decision, Tage?" asked Fru Fønss.

"I can't believe you doubt me. Just imagine our
family life: Ida and I sitting out there on the terrace on
a moonlit night, and someone whispers behind the
laurel bush, and Ida asks me who's whispering, and I
reply: 'It's my mother and her new husband.' No, no,
I shouldn't have said that; but you see already how it
would look, what anguish it has caused me, and it
won't be any better for Ellinor, believe me."

Fru Fønss let her children go and sat there alone.

No, Tage was right, it hadn't been good for them.
How far apart they had already grown in one short
hour; how they looked at her, not as her children, but
as their father's children, and how ready they were to
let her go as soon as they noticed that not every feeling
in her heart belonged to them; but she was not merely
Tage's and Ellinor's mother, she was a separate person
with her own life and hopes that had no connection to
them. But perhaps she was not as young as she had
thought. She felt it in the conversation with her children. Hadn't she sat there, fearful in spite of her
words, feeling almost like someone who had en-
croached upon the rights of youth, and hadn't all the
confident importunity of youth and its naïve tyranny
permeated everything *they* had said? We are the ones

who deserve your love, it is to *us* that life belongs, and your life is to exist for us.

She began to understand that it might be a relief to be quite old; not that she wished for this, but it smiled at her faintly like a distant peace after all the turmoil she had recently been through, and now that the prospect of so much discord was at hand. For she did not believe that her children would change the views they held, and yet she would have to discuss them over and over again before she gave up hope. The best thing was that Thorbrøgger was going to leave at once; when he was no longer present the children might be less irritable and she might be able to show them how eager she was to give them all possible consideration; the first bitterness would have time to subside and everything... no, she did not believe that everything would be fine.

As it turned out, Thorbrøgger consented to travel to Denmark to put their papers in order. For the time being, she would remain behind. Nothing seemed to have been gained by this, however. The children shunned her; Tage was constantly with Ida or her father, and Ellinor was always keeping the ill Fru Kastager company. And whenever they were finally together, what had happened to the old intimacy, the old coziness, and where were the thousands of topics of conversation? And when they finally found one, what had become of its fascination? They would sit there, keeping the conversation going the way people do who have enjoyed each other's company for some time and are now about to part, and the ones who are leaving have all their thoughts concentrated on the goal of their journey, while the ones who will stay behind are thinking only of how they will slip back into a familiar life and familiar routines as soon as the strangers have left.

There was no sense of community in their lives anymore, all feeling of belonging together had vanished. They might talk about arrangements for next week, next month, or the months after that, but it did not interest them as days of their own lives; it was simply a matter of a waiting period that had to be endured one way or another, for all three of them asked themselves: Then what? Because they felt no security in their lives, because they had no reason to make plans before *it* was taken care of, the thing that had divided them.

And for each day that passed, the children forgot more and more what their mother had meant to them, as children will do when they think they have been wronged; thousands of kindnesses were forgotten for one injustice.

Tage was the more sensitive of the two, but also the one more deeply wounded because he was the one who had loved the most. He had wept long nights over the mother he could not keep exactly the way he wished, and there were times when the memory of her love for him was about to smother all other feeling in his breast. One day he went to her and begged and pleaded for her to be theirs, theirs alone and no one else's, but he received a "no." And this "no" had made him bitter, and cold too, a coldness that frightened him at first because it brought with it such a terrible emptiness.

Things were different for Ellinor; in an odd way she had felt it largely as an injustice toward her deceased father, and she began an obsessive worship of the father she only dimly could remember, and she made him seem so alive by immersing herself in everything she had heard about him; she asked Kastager about him, and Tage; every morning and evening she kissed a portrait medallion of him that she had, longing almost hysterically for letters from him that were still at home, and for things that had belonged to him.

At the same time that her father rose, her mother sank. The fact that she had fallen in love with a man diminished her in her daughter's eyes; she was no longer the mother, the infallible, the most wise, the best, the most beautiful; she was a female like other women, not perfect, but because she was not perfect, she was someone who could be criticized and judged, in whom weaknesses and faults could be found. Ellinor was glad that she had not confided in her mother about her unrequited love; but she had no idea to what extent it was her mother who had prevented her from doing so.

One day passed and then the next, and life grew more and more intolerable, and all three of them felt that it was fruitless, and that instead of drawing them together, it was driving them apart.

Fru Kastager, who had now recovered, had not participated in any of what had happened, but was nevertheless the one among them with the best perspective on things, since she had been told everything. One day she had a long conversation with Fru Fønss, who was happy to have someone who could listen calmly to how she imagined the future; and during that conversation Fru Kastager suggested that the children should travel with her to Nice, that Thorbrøgger be summoned to Avignon, and that they should be married. Herr Kastager could stay behind to act as their witness.

Fru Fønss wavered for some time, for it was impossible for her to discover what the children thought; when they were told, they received the news with dignified silence, and when they were pressed for a response, they simply said that in this matter they would, of course, comply with whatever she decided.

And so things were arranged as Fru Kastager had proposed. Fru Fønss said goodbye to her children and they departed; Thorbrøgger arrived and they were married.

Spain became their home; Thorbrøgger chose it because of the sheep-raising.

Neither of them wanted to return to Denmark.

And so they lived happily in Spain.

A few times she wrote to her children, but in their initial fierce wrath over the fact that she had abandoned them, they sent her letters back. Later they probably regretted this but could not make themselves admit it by writing to her, and so all ties between them were severed. But occasionally they would hear, through other people, about each other's lives.

For five years Thorbrøgger and his wife lived happily, but suddenly she fell ill. It was a rapidly ravaging disease that could only end in death. Her strength vanished by the hour, and one day when the grave was no longer far away, she wrote to her children:

> Dear Children,
>
> I know that you will read this letter, for it will not reach you until I am dead. Don't worry, there are no reproaches concealed in these lines; if only I could make them contain enough love!
>
> When people love, Tage and Ellinor, little Ellinor, the one who loves most must humble himself, and that is why I come to you once

more, as I will come to you in my thoughts
every hour of the day for as long as I can. The
one who must die, dear children, is so bereft; I
am so impoverished, because this entire lovely
world, which for so many years has been my
rich, blessed home, is to be taken from me; my
chair will stand empty, the door will close on
me, and I shall never set foot here again. This is
why I look on all the world with the prayer in
my eyes that it will care for me, this is why I
come and implore you to love me with all the
love you once gave me; don't forget, to be remembered is the only part of the human world
that will be mine from now on. Simply to be
remembered, nothing more.

I have never doubted your love, I fully understood that it was your great love that provoked
your great anger; had you loved me less, you
would have let me go more easily. And that is
why I want to say that if one day a man, bowed
with sorrow, should come to your door to talk
to you about me, to talk about me for the sake
of his own consolation, then you must remember that no one has loved me as he has, and all
the happiness that can stream from one person's heart to another has passed from him to
me. And soon, in the last great hour, he will

hold my hand when the darkness comes, and his words will be the last that I hear...

Farewell, I say here, but this is not my last farewell to you; that I will utter as late as I dare, and it will hold all my love, and longings from many many years, and memories from the days when you were small, and a thousand wishes and a thousand thanks. Farewell, Tage. Farewell, Ellinor. Farewell until the last farewell.

Your Mother.

Afterword

There are moments in my life when I believe that the study of Nature is my life's calling; but at other times it seems as if poetry should be my vocation, and this occurs precisely when some fine poem has aroused my enthusiasm or when I have been reading Nordic mythology. If I could transfer Nature's eternal laws, its delights, mysteries, and miracles into the world of poetry, then I feel that my work would become more than commonplace.

Jens Peter Jacobsen
January 15, 1867

At the age of twenty, Jens Peter Jacobsen was torn between the two great passions of his life: science and poetry. He was an ardent botanist, and there was nothing he enjoyed more than "botanizing" along the shores of the Limfjord or in the marshes near his childhood home in Thisted. His first published work was a botanical essay, which appeared in 1870 in the journal *Nyt dansk Maanedsskrift* (New Danish Monthly), edited by Vilhelm Møller, who was to remain a lifelong friend. And for the next four years Jacobsen devoted much of his time to translating into

Danish the monumental works of Darwin, *On the Origin of Species* and *The Descent of Man*. He also published several articles explaining Darwin's theories, and thus made the radical new ideas accessible to the general Danish public for the first time. In 1873 he won the University of Copenhagen's prestigious gold medal for his treatise on freshwater algae, and he had plans to write a doctoral thesis, as well as a book on the plant life of Denmark.

But Jacobsen's scientific fervor was matched by his great love of poetry. He had written verse since the age of nine, and in 1869 he tried in vain to find a publisher for his first collections of poems. Even the critic Georg Brandes, who was the foremost spokesperson for the new, groundbreaking literary ideas of the time, failed to recognize Jacobsen's talent in these early poems. In fact, it was only with the posthumous publication of his poetry that Jacobsen's poetic genius was discovered. And so his literary debut was not as a poet, but as the author of the novella "Mogens."

During the spring of 1872, Jacobsen worked on the story that he had promised for Vilhelm Møller's journal. Slowly, with long intervals between sentences, but unperturbed by his editor's impatience or his friends' teasing, Jacobsen filled odd-sized, multicolored sheets of paper that were then wrested from him, one by one, and carried off to the printer. Once the pages were sent off he made no changes, and his superb memory allowed him to submit the pages without keeping a draft while he finished the story. His slow pace was not the result of laziness, however; with his keen sense of language and profound respect for the power of words—regarding them almost as living organisms—he would meticulously search for precisely the right turn of phrase. Edvard Brandes (Georg's brother and Jacobsen's close friend) wrote years later that Jacobsen would have vehemently opposed restoring the ordinary syntax to the opening line of "Mogens." As Brandes said, all of the language, the

poetry, the atmosphere, and the tone would collapse if it said
"It was summer..." instead of "Summer it was...." Jacobsen had
a penchant for reading dictionaries, and he made lists of long-
forgotten words and expressions that might someday prove use-
ful. When he was writing, he was capable of deep concentration;
he took no notice of the passage of time.

When "Mogens" appeared in *Nyt dansk Maanedsskrift*, the
leading critics immediately acknowledged that the story, with its
beautifully lyrical opening passages, marked an extraordinary
turning point in Danish literature—its naturalistic style and
atheistic tendencies were entirely new. Both Brandes brothers
realized that with this story the gangly, awkward young man
from the provinces had placed himself in the forefront of what
became known as the "Modern Breakthrough." He had indeed
managed to "transfer Nature's eternal laws, its delights, mysteries, and miracles" into his writing.

After the publication of "Mogens," Jacobsen worked on
his first novel, *Marie Grubbe*, while continuing to lead a rather
bohemian existence in Copenhagen. He would get up at noon,
wander around the city, eat an inexpensive meal at the Student
Club, and then return to his spartan one-room lodgings to work.
At 9 o'clock he would go out to spend the evening in a café with
friends, who knew him as a cheerful and fun-loving young man,
full of the oddest caprices. His one affectation was his fondness
for his top hat, which he wore everywhere and which later won
him the nickname "Excellency." Then he would return to his
room and read until the early morning hours. He read the sagas,
Taine, Mill, Hans Christian Andersen, Kierkegaard, Dickens,
Shakespeare, Tennyson, and Edgar Allen Poe. He also read vast
quantities of popular literature, especially the English "gov-
erness novels," from which he said he gleaned an understanding
of people. Jacobsen diligently kept track of how many pages he
had read, the number reaching as high as 10,000 pages a month
while he was working on *Marie Grubbe*.

In 1874, after finishing two chapters of his novel, which
was to be an overnight sensation when it appeared two years
later (the news of its erotic content causing it to sell out within
days), Jacobsen set off for a long trip through Germany, Austria,
and Italy. In Venice he suddenly fell ill, and in Florence he suffered a hemorrhage which prompted him to cut short his trip
and return at once to his family home in Thisted. There he was
given the fateful news that he was in the advanced stages of
tuberculosis, with little hope for a cure. At the age of twenty-
seven, his scientific career was definitively over, but for eleven
and a half years Jacobsen clung fiercely to life and managed to
write some of the most exquisite prose ever produced.

While he slowly worked on his two novels (creating his
masterpiece, *Niels Lyhne*, at an excruciating pace, sometimes
taking six months to write only seven lines), Jacobsen also wrote
short stories. In 1875 he finished "A Shot in the Fog," a Poe-
inspired story of a man doomed by sadistic acts of revenge and
subsequent guilt. In 1879 "Two Worlds" appeared, written during the author's third and last trip abroad to Germany, Rome,
and Montreux. From 1881 until the summer of 1884, Jacobsen
lived once again in his beloved Copenhagen, returning to
Thisted to rest whenever his illness overwhelmed him. The two
stories "There Should Have Been Roses" and "The Plague in
Bergamo" were both completed in 1881.

A year later he wrote "Fru Fønss," as *Mogens and Other
Stories* was waiting at the printer. Edvard Brandes recalled that
Jacobsen took even longer than usual to finish the story and he
seemed especially loath to write the last pages, which would con-
tain Fru Fønss's farewell letter to her children: "Finally one
morning, he wrote it without stopping, all in one piece—as he
wept. Jacobsen himself confessed with much levity that he had
'grown sentimental' over his own lovely words, but, he added,
'It *is* touching.' And his friends obligingly laughed, although
they all knew that with these words Jacobsen had written his

farewell to the world and was urging those who were fond of him to remember him."

In July of 1884, Jacobsen left Copenhagen for the last time. On April 30, 1885 he died in Thisted, meeting death with resolute calm and dignity—a scientist, atheist, and poet to the end.

The writings of Jens Peter Jacobsen, though few in number, have had a profound influence on some of the most celebrated authors of this century. It is hoped that with these new translations of his stories, his great literary legacy will not be forgotten.

Tiina Nunnally
Seattle, January 1994

References

Breve fra J. P. Jacobsen. Edited and with a foreword by Edvard Brandes. Copenhagen: Gyldendal, 1899.

Samlede Værker, Vols. 5 & 6. J. P. Jacobsen. Copenhagen: Rosenkilde og Bagger, 1973.

Dansk Litteraturhistorie, Vol. 4. Copenhagen: Politikens Forlag, 1977.

Dansk Litteraturhistorie, Vol. 6. Copenhagen: Gyldendal, 1985.

Lyrik og prosa. J. P. Jacobsen. Edited and with an afterword by Jørgen Erslev Andersen. Danske Klassikere, Det danske Sprog- og Litteraturselskab. Copenhagen: Borgen, 1993.

Fjord Modern Classics

No. 1

Pelle the Conqueror, Volume 1: Childhood
by Martin Andersen Nexø
Translated by Steven T. Murray

No. 2

Niels Lyhne
by Jens Peter Jacobsen
Translated by Tiina Nunnally

No. 3

Katinka
by Herman Bang
Translated by Tiina Nunnally

No. 4

Pelle the Conqueror, Volume 2: Apprenticeship
by Martin Andersen Nexø
Translated by Steven T. Murray & Tiina Nunnally

No. 5

Mogens and Other Stories
by Jens Peter Jacobsen
Translated by Tiina Nunnally